The Bond Series

Book 1

THE ROYAL
BOND

Keylee Hargis

The Bond Series Book 1

THE ROYAL BOND

ISBN: 978-1-7359207-0-2

First Edition: 2020

Printed in the United States.

To all my readers from Wattpad,

this wouldn't be possible without you.

CHAPTER ONE

—◆◇◆—

Scarlett

I ran as fast as my legs could take me. The growls sounded throughout the forest, bouncing off the trees, *taunting* me. They were surrounding me, and I had no clue where to go. My paws hit the ground harder as I forced my wolf to a sprint, taking her beyond her limits as her soft whimpers echoed around in my mind.

The growls grew fainter, and I realized I was losing them. Spotting a river ahead, I jumped in and began swimming quickly across it, hoping my scent would get lost in the flow of the water.

On the other side, I jumped out and as I kept running, my wolf began to slow, needing to rest. I took over control, shifting mid-walk, bare for all to see. I bolted towards the small, yet familiar cottage and opened the door, slipping in and locking it behind me, panting heavily. Still on guard, I threw on some clothes and collapsed onto my bed, exhausted from the chase.

Phew, I need to run more.

"What have you done now?"

Startled, I bolted up and turned to see my younger sister leaning up against the doorframe of my bedroom. Relieved it was just her; I slumped back down to my previous spot.

"I stole some bread from the market," I answered as I heard her sigh exasperatedly.

"How many times have mom and dad told you? We don't steal! They'll be furious if they find out!"

Shaking my head, I leveled my sister with an irritated look. "I was hungry, Ashlee!"

She flinched from my heated voice. "I know," Ashlee lamented, "We all are, but being in the sectors puts us in that position. We just have to have hope— just like mom and dad tell us to." with that, she held a glint of that so-called hope in her eyes, causing me to scoff.

"Hope for what exactly?" I looked away and down at my dirty hands, feeling the sting of a glare building up behind my eyes. "I clean people's houses for money, dad works in the mines, and mom -" I furrowed my eyebrows, shooting my gaze back up at my sister, "Well, mom can barely even sew for her job anymore. Face it; *we're poor!* No one will accept us into a pack, and they sure as hell don't care about the sectors! They aren't bringing people up anymore! I've prayed to our Moon Goddess, and I know when it's time to give up."

I stood to my feet, shaking my head again as she stared intensely back at me. Biting the inside of my cheek, I brought my hand up and pointed a finger at Ashlee's chest, almost poking her.

"And you should too, Ashlee. We're at the bottom of the food chain, and there's nothing we can do about it. I admire your strength and hope, but you're too young to understand." I gave her one final glance before brushing past her and heading towards the kitchen.

"I'm sixteen!" She countered from the other room, but I ignored her.

My stomach rumbled, bringing me back to the situation with the bread earlier. I was just so hungry that I couldn't help myself. I growled, annoyed. How come the packs get to live in luxury, and we, the sectors, are left to suffer?

In our country, our lives are dictated by the Personal Status System. It started in the states after the last brutal war broke out between the wolves and the witches. The witches declared war on wolves for dominating the world, breaking the peace treaty we had in place with them. In short, they hated us.

At a young age, I could never understand why, but now the humans ruled under the wolves' command, and the witches had no say. They regretted making us— creating us. Could there not have been another way?

The monarchy started when the most prosperous family decided it was time for a change. They found a witch that agreed to help them perform some very profound, dark magic, resulting in the creation of the Royal Family. The King's pack destroyed the witches, completely wiping them out. At the time, rumors surfaced that the royals had the help of an unknown witch — a witch that, still to this day, no one could identify. I never knew why she helped them. I had always thought it was a myth or legend and still kind of do in some ways.

There are three main packs that people strive to be in: War, Power, and Intelligence. Each pack is led by a strong leader we call the Alpha.

If you're not in any of the top packs, you're at the bottom — inadequate, useless, and seen as weak — forced to live life in the sectors, or just sectioned off land, with no chance at advancing into a pack. These lands are used for the sole purpose of keeping "poor people" away from the real packs and, most importantly, apart from the royal family. Sickness was a big issue in the sectors, too. Because we weren't given medical support, it was easy to say we were no strangers to death.

The Royal Pack, or as I like to call them, The Golden Pack, are at the top of the food chain. The best of the best. You have to be born a royal even to be considered a part of the pack. Unless you're a servant, you don't even get to look at the palace. The King, the all-powerful and mighty Alpha Christian, the one whose elders banished us all to the PS system, runs it.

He's the Alpha King—the alpha of all alphas.

Because of his elders, the sectors are at the bottom, and we're continuously put in our place. We work our asses off, and barely ever get rewarded for it. *I hate it.*

The front door swung wide open, shattering my thoughts, revealing an angry mother and father.

"Scarlett Rose Madison, come here *now*!" My father's voice boomed. *Oh no.*

I exited the kitchen and came into their view.

"Care to explain yourself?"

Act dumb.

"Explain what?" I shrugged innocently.

"Oh, don't you play that game with me, chica. I know what you did today at the market. Don't make me get *la chancla*!" My mother barked, pointing her finger accusingly at me, and my eyes widened at the threat of a whack of her flip flop.

"Okay, *okay!* I stole a piece of bread, so what?" I asked, folding my arms, trying to play it off.

"No! Not only did you *just* steal a piece of bread, but you also *ran* from pack police! You resisted arrest! What were you even doing near the Intelligence Pack? Are you crazy?"

"I had to clean a house! I was near the market, and I was hungry. I hadn't eaten in almost two days! I just lost my self-control walking past all the food, that's all."

My father dug into his pocket and shoved a piece of paper into my hands. My mother gave me a sad look. She knew I was hungry, and I know that she felt it was her fault, though it wasn't. It was just the world we lived in.

I would never blame her for it.

"You committed a crime, Scarlett, and it's dire. Forget the bread; you ran from pack police. You can't do that."

I straightened the piece of paper my father handed to me, and my eyes nearly shot out of my head as I read it.

"A fine?!" I yelled incredulously.

"Yeah, they lost you, so they found us—*your parents*. Did you ever stop to think about that?" Mother asked softly.

"Two hundred dollars," I mumbled, guilt rising in my throat like a thick lump.

"You also have a court hearing for resisting arrest. I hope you're happy. Not only are we even more in debt, but you have to go to the Intelligence Pack for your hearing. Who knows what will happen! Goddess, this will be bad for your business," Dad muttered, walking towards a cabinet in our kitchen he goes to when he feels like drinking his life away.

"I have a court hearing over a piece of bread, and you're worried about *business?*"

"You resisted arrest! The fine isn't about the damn bread!" He yelled as I flinched, staggering back a bit.

"You got yourself into this, now get yourself out of it. You're lucky the pack police didn't follow us here and arrest you for good measure. Now go get cleaned up while I try to scramble something together for dinner."

My mom gave me one more of her suffering looks, furthermore, elevating my guilt, and turned her back to me. I looked down at the floor and trudged towards my room with my tail tucked between my legs. My sister stood nearby with a smug look on her face as if to say, 'I told you so.' Annoyed, I growled, baring my teeth at her. The once smug look slipped off her face as she moved back into her room.

That's what I thought.

"Act human for once, please!" My father yelled out, and I rolled my eyes, shutting my door behind me, maybe slamming it just a bit.

"I'm not human, you big oaf," I muttered to myself, angrily kicking a box on the floor.

CHAPTER TWO

---◆◇◆---

Scarlett

"At least make yourself look presentable," Mother scolded, trying to pat down my hair as I fought with her, pushing her hands away as we whispered to each other angrily.

"Enough!" My father hissed.

I looked around as people from the Intelligence Pack eyed us as if we were aliens. At the sight, Mom immediately pulled away from my hair, smoothing her shirt out as if that was going to make her look any less like she was from the sectors. I growled lowly, causing them to look away.

We made our way to the courthouse, at the center of the pack, where the hearing would be held. As we walked down the street filled with immaculately dressed people, the seriousness of this all finally hit me. I didn't want to go to pack jail! I was too young to be cooped up in a cell. When we got to the front of the courthouse, guards stalked out to meet us and took me by the arms.

"Hey! What are you doing? Let go!" I struggled, trying to break free, but it was no use. It only made their grip tighter.

"It's just a precaution, calm down. We're taking you to your seat. You are untrustworthy as of right now," the guard gruffly told me, glaring at me as if I was already guilty and sentenced.

"It was a chunk of bread!" I practically whined out.

"It was *resisting* arrest." the guard snapped, and I looked up only to fight back a grin. He was one of the wolves I ran from the day of the chase.

Ha, *too slow.*

Reluctantly, I stopped my thrashing and went with them, glancing back at my parents, who were following close behind. This was so embarrassing. It was *bread!* Sure, I ran from the police, but a lot of people do— it's on the TV all the time. So what? *So, you're delusional,* my subconscious spoke.

As the massive mahogany doors opened before me, people stood and waited for me to take my seat. Wow. They're going all out for a piece of bread. I should applaud them and their audacity.

Once I was seated, my parents sat behind me with other pack members who wanted something to gossip about to fulfil their own boring lives.

"All rise," the judge announced, his hands raised with an authentic look that made my nose wrinkle in distaste.

So many people in power that think they can hold it over people like me.

I glanced around as everyone stood, and the judge directed his attention towards me.

"Oh, *oh!*" I quickly rose to my feet and stood, my cheeks turning a light pink. *Now's not the time to get all preachy, Scarlett.*

After a moment, everyone sat back down, and someone came to sit next to me as the judge talked to the guards.

"I'm your attorney," the woman smiled. My eyes widened at her. *I can't pay for this.*

"Don't worry. It's your basic right to one, even if you can't afford it," She reassured, setting out papers from her briefcase.

"This is so stupid, bread? Really?" She mumbled to herself.

"Thank you!" I erupted, throwing my hands in the air exasperatedly. Everyone looked at me once more, causing me to sink back into my seat.

My attorney rose from her seat, stalking up to the judge, handing him a paper, and talking to him with the other attorney. They seemed to be in a heated discussion as their voices kept rising until practically half of the courtroom could hear their conversation.

"That's absurd!" the persecutor claimed while the woman shrugged.

"You're trying to make a young girl from the sectors pay a *two hundred dollar* fine? She was scared, and she ran, it happens. It would be different if she were caught stealing jewelry or selling drugs, but a *chunk* of bread? Do you have no compassion?" She snapped.

The judge clasped his fingers together, resting them in front of himself, and looked between the two lawyers. Finally, after a second of deliberation, the old man spoke up, "I'll allow it. I'll contact him. Besides, I agree with the girl. It's stupid to waste the court's time and resources for such a petty charge."

My attorney smirked, walking back to her seat with a smug look.

"What did you just request?" I asked eagerly.

She took her seat, her hands rustling with some documents. "That I speak to the Alpha for a plea deal. His people are putting civilians in court over the most stupid things now. They're just looking for trouble and people's money. For instance, one person was cleaning and scratched a floor, so, of course, the owners demanded to see them in court," She scowled, setting the papers down with a heavy sigh, "I don't understand this pack anymore."

I licked my lips, leaning towards her. "Why call the Alpha here for such a small hearing, though?"

"Maybe if I keep calling him down here, he'll stop these stupid little trials and get a new managing system!" She growled out.

"You seem to know him well to request him like that?"

"I'm his sister."

For a second time since finding out this woman was my attorney, my eyes widened, and I was about to question why she was an attorney when she was the alpha's sister, but I thought against it. It wasn't my business. Besides, I was way below her in rank.

Minutes later, the doors opened, and I knew he had arrived from the power that radiated into the room. Followed by a band of lower-ranking officers, probably as his assistants, he made his way towards us.

"Sister, why have you called me here again?" He demanded.

As I laid my eyes on him, I never knew how handsome someone could be. *Like seriously!* I could stare at him all day, but before anyone could catch me, I looked away quickly, feeling the slow burn of a blush crawling up my neck out of embarrassment.

He continued to stare his sister down, obviously still annoyed, and ignoring me.

"Do you know what this trial was about?" She questioned him, and he shook his head.

"I don't know. Did this woman attack someone or something?" He halfheartedly asked, looking at me now. I made myself look back at him, too, but I felt like an ant under his stare.

"No. *Scarlett*— that's her name, by the way, stole a piece of *bread*. Literally, like a *chunk*," She emphasized, and the other attorney began to protest, but not long before the alpha held up his hand, silencing him.

I looked around as his pack members stood star-struck by him as if they were graced to be in his presence. People even gathered at the back doors— I guess their alpha was like a celebrity to them.

Are all alphas of our nation's packs celebrities?

"You're telling me," the Alpha started, placing his hands on his hips and looking around the silent courtroom, "all of this was over a piece of bread?" His sister nodded. He then ran one of his hands over his face and sighed. "What is this pack coming to?"

"*Yes*! Your people keep bringing the dumbest cases into the court! A small fine would be appropriate or community service even! They're wasting everyone's time by continuously bringing these petty cases here."

You go, girl! My lips pulled into a small smirk before I could stop myself.

"She ran from the pack police! She resisted arrest! It's illegal..." the other attorney blurted out.

I squinted my eyes at him— *what a snitch.*

The alpha gazed at me briefly and turned towards the judge. "How much was the fine? What is the letter of her sector? And is there any history with pack police?"

Again with this ignoring my existence?

"Two hundred dollar fine, and she resides in sector C. She also has no criminal history." He answered respectfully, bowing his head.

The alpha's face twisted into a look that just screamed 'done' as he looked up at the judge. "Drop the fine completely and order community service. No one should be put on trial for being hungry. The service is for resisting arrest. This is a warning," He then turned to back toward his sister, but pointed at one of his men. "Call Melissa, I want to talk with her and our pack police, and someone, for the sake of all that is *right and holy* in this world, please send some food to the sectors! I'll pay for it." He ordered.

"You." His attention was now on his sister. "Follow me. You're going to learn to stop pulling me from meetings. How many times have I told you? Only call for me if it's life or death."

What a charmer.

I turned and faced my mom, catching sight of her relieved smile. She held my dad's hand with an air of gratitude surrounding both of them, and I just shrugged one shoulder in an 'I don't know what just happened, but I'm happy' kind of way.

"Everyone is dismissed." the Alpha called out before heading for the doors.

"You are one lucky son of a gun," My father stated. I nodded but hardly listened to him as I watched Mr. Alpha walk out of the courtroom, his followers right at his heels.

"I don't even want to think about what my community service will be," I grumbled

"Don't even try to complain. It could've been so much worse," Mom snapped.

That freaking chunk of bread.

CHAPTER THREE

◆◇◆

Scarlett

I stared at the thin paper, clenched tightly between my fingers with disgust.

"This is ridiculous!" I groaned before Ashlee snatched the paper from my hands, skimming over it and beginning to laugh. I tried to reach for the document but missed as she threw her hand down to give me a taunting smirk.

"You have to do *community service* at The War Pack? That *blows*," She mocked, only allowing herself a pinch of pity for her *poor sister*. I only glared back at the brat, considering clawing her eyes out. *So very tempting.*

As she noticed my sadistic stare, she took a step backward. Ever since her thirteenth birthday party, she'd always been a little scared of me. Some boy—a real mangy pup—had tried to kiss her, and I tackled him so quickly that I broke a few of his ribs and bruised his face—only a little—although, in my defense, he was two years older than her. I wasn't just going to let him kiss her!

"Looks like you're going to be gone for a bit," Mom stated, handing me a bag.

"You're enjoying this!" I exclaimed, and she shrugged.

"Sí. You were going to get caught for the little things you did eventually, and now you have. I believe a week or two in The War Pack will be good for you, Mija!"

I threw one of my hands up and slapped my forehead in disbelief. "Mom, it's *The War Pack*. It's where the scariest of fighters are, and it's where all the prisoners are just *ready* to break free and kill anyone they see! It's the most terrifying pack there is! I don't deserve this! It's not like I killed anyone!"

"Stop whining. You're giving me a headache," My father called from the living room, where he was sipping his whiskey as he always does whenever something *important* is happening, which is all of the time. *Glad to know why our money is always gone. How about you stop drinking our money away?!*

"Yeah," Ashlee piped in again, "look on the bright side, you're just cleaning the Alpha's mansion for the week with other maids, so it could've been worse. Plus, you could get to see Alpha Mason. *Yummy*." She then started practically drooling as she stared off into space with a dreamy grin. I gaped at her as my mom rolled up her newspaper, whacking it over the back of my sister's head.

"Ow!"

"You're sixteen! Act like it. Dios mío," My mother snapped, and I grinned, but it immediately dropped as she turned towards me.

"And *you* get packing! Your ride will be here within the hour." I grimaced at the thought and sighed, dragging myself back to my room with the bag my mother gave me.

***

I watched the scenery go by as I sat in the back of the small car. The driver had not spoken a single word since he had picked me up. You could tell he was a War Pack member by the tribal tattoo snaking down his arm—all males in the army were supposed to have one. I tried to get my mind off the War Pack. Of all the stories I've heard, not a single one has forgotten to mention that Alpha Mason is vicious when he wants to be.

The War Pack was about an hour or two away from where I lived, so since I had time to kill, I slept. It wasn't like I had anyone to talk to or anything better to do in the tiny car.

Later, after a somewhat blissful sleep, I was shaken awake by my driver. I looked around, realizing that we'd made it. Just outside the car window, I could see that we were parked in front of a vast mansion. My heart leaped as I gawked at it.

It was elegant yet scary.

My driver had my bags in his hands and motioned me out. I did as I was told and scrambled out, shutting the door behind me. Moments later, we walked to the front doors, where two guards opened them and ushered us through.

Minutes after our arrival, a sharp-dressed woman walked up to us looking professional and like she belonged in this mansion, unlike me in my pair of worn-out jeans and cheap t-shirt.

"Good afternoon, you must be Scarlett Madison."

I nodded, and she smiled, motioning for me to follow her. I took my bags from my driver and hurried after her retreating figure.

"I must admit, when I heard your story, I couldn't help but be confused." She mentioned.

My brows furrowed. "Why?"

"You stole bread? You ran for stealing a chunk of bread, but why not just let them arrest you? It would've only been a small fine. Resisting made it worse."

Again, with the freaking bread.

I kept my eyes on the woman as we walked farther into the mansion, maybe to pierce her thick head with my imaginary dagger, or to understand where she was coming from, I couldn't decide. Still, I ended up choosing to enlighten her with my most honest answer.

"I don't understand why that is so weird? When you're hungry, you'll do a lot of things, maybe worse than stealing bread." She didn't look too convinced—probably because she'd never understand what being hungry felt like—so I delved further. "I've seen people get *killed* fighting over a *bowl of soup*. I ran because I couldn't afford to stay and risk getting the fine, but it found its way back to me anyways." The woman finally seemed to understand as she led me up a flight of stairs.

"Well, I can assure you that as long as you're here, you won't be hungry."

That's the best thing I've heard all day.

"Maybe I should try to get community service more often," I joked, trying to lighten the mood, and she let out a small laugh.

Maybe she isn't as posh as I thought.

"I'm Elizabeth," She finally introduced, and I smiled back at her.

"It's nice to meet you," We came to a door, and she put in a key, unlocking it and swung the door open.

"Here is your room. It's a bit small, but you'll only sleep in here, so it's perfect for the job. You have a bathroom connected through that door right there." I nodded, thanking her, and stepped in, setting my things down.

"You don't fully start until tomorrow, so make yourself at home. I'll come to get you before dinner. Feel free to explore a little. If anyone asks, tell them that I permitted you to. However, I ask that you do not go upstairs to the very top level. That's the Alpha's floor. See you later." With that said, she was gone, and I looked around my new accommodations.

"I guess I could unpack first," I whispered to myself, so that's what I did. I spent a good hour or so unpacking and just setting things up how I liked. Even if I were going to be here for a week or two, I wanted to be comfortable. As I looked around at my handy work, I thought to myself that maybe this wouldn't be so bad.

***

I spoke too soon.

I was currently lost. This place was enormous! I should have never left my room to explore. In all honesty, I should have left some breadcrumbs— *oh the irony.*

I growled, annoyed at everything as I made the same turn from a few minutes ago *again.*

I found a staircase a moment later, and I started to descend it, going down a level.

Okay, I think we're getting somewhere here.

I walked down this random hallway, just minding my own business when a door burst open. An angry man rushed out, knocking the first guard on duty, that I've seen for the *first time* since taking my little journey through this labyrinth, out cold.

"Show yourself Mason!" the man bellowed, and I froze, my eyes wide and shoulders tense.

Is this one of the prisoners I've feared meeting? Is he a murderer? Is he here for me?!

His attention shifted to me.

Oh, *hell* no!

"Where is your Alpha?" He asked, marching over to me as I stood puzzled.

Oh yeah! He wants Alpha Mason, not me. Phew.

I pursed my lips, shrugging my shoulders with my hands raised. "I uh, I don't know? I'm not a member," I stated, and he laughed humorlessly, grabbing me by the arm.

"Don't play games with me!" He snarled.

"I stole bread, and I'm here for community service! He's not my Alpha! I'm not lying!" I yelled out, squeezing my eyes shut as sudden fear started to envelop my thoughts.

A moment passed of complete utter silence before I opened my eyes again and saw the man staring at me in utter confusion.

"You're lying," He tried again, but he seemed to be trying to figure me out.

I let out a nervous laugh to try and lighten the mood. "No, actually I'm not," But then my temper started taking over, and I ground out, "When a gigantic oaf is manhandling you and screaming in your face, you tend to tell the truth."

He growled at me again, a bit angrier than before, and I mentally cursed myself for opening my big mouth.

"Never mind that. You must know where he is since you're here on community service. He had to accept your arrival into the pack for the time being."

When the criminal started pulling me with him down the hall, I couldn't help but whimper. His grip was like a vice, and there was no escaping it. "Ow, you're hurting me!" I cried, but he only laughed.

"I don't care. Mason always likes the ones in distress. Now scream, and let's see if he comes to your rescue."

"What?" I asked dumbly. Is this man insane? *Clearly*, I decided, but when he partially shifted—turning into a half-wolf, half-human *monster*—and roared right into my face, I knew for sure that he was a clinical psychopath. And as quickly as it came, what little courage I had mustered left me, and I screamed. Loudly, might I add. I've only ever seen my father partially shift once before when he got angry. It takes a lot of strength even to be able to *do it*, let alone have self-control while doing so.

"Good," He murmured, shifting back into his regular features. My heartbeat had spiked, and I was breathing heavily.

"Why do I have so much bad luck?" I muttered as he continued to drag me down the hall, his grip bruising, and his face contorted into a furious scowl. With all this bad juju, I really shouldn't have had the gall to test it, but I couldn't help it. I just wanted to escape from the whole situation, and me being me, I just had to try. "Hey, so do you uh know how to get back to hall B?"

"Shut up!" He growled viciously.

"Okay," I squeaked. *It was worth a shot*, my subconscious spoke.

Suddenly, the air shifted, and a booming voice growled almost as viciously as the criminal had. "Let her go!"

The man halted in his pursuit and turned us both around to see who had caught him, causing me to almost fall over in the process.

"Now!" the new man added dangerously.

"Mason," My assailant grinned.

I steadied myself with my free hand, clutching at the man's bulging bicep for support and lifted my eyes to see who precisely this Alpha Mason was. My eyes widened at the man standing before the criminal and me. Were all alpha's hot and intimidating? *He looked like a Greek God.*

"Let the girl go. *Now*," Alpha Mason repeated.

"Or what?" the man asked.

Alpha Mason took a step forward, and I stood in shock at what he did next. I didn't know whether to find him terrifying when he roared, with his eyes shining a bright red and the sound reverberating through my ribs, or attractive.

Really, Scar? Again, with the wrong timing!

"You wanted me; I'm here. Now let her go! She's not part of this." Alpha Mason countered, and the man looked down at me with a bone-chilling smirk.

I narrowed my eyes in both a silent plea and a challenge.

"I don't think so," He tightened his grip on me, causing my heart to speed up to an even faster rate. I could feel my flight or fight senses kicking in, and me being me, I did something I knew I'd regret later—I head-butted him.

"Shiitake Mushrooms!" I cried out, holding my bruised nose. "That was so much more badass in my head," I muttered, stumbling out of the insane man's grasp as he held his nose, groaning— Well, no, more like screaming in rage.

A hand curled around my shoulder, gripping my shirt and pulling me behind them. I stood shocked, once again, as Alpha Mason took on a protective stance before me.

"Run," He ordered.

"Run? What about you?!" I spluttered.

He laughed at the suggestion. "This pup? *Please...* Don't worry about me."

That was all I needed before mumbling a quick '*have fun*' and darting down the hall. I rounded the corner and grinned at what was before me. "My room," I dramatically yelled as I shut myself in quickly, locking the door.

How do I, Scarlett Madison, find myself in the most horrific situations? Am I a magnet for trouble or something?

After a while, there was a loud knock on my door. I jumped and quickly looked around nervously for something to use as protection. *What if it's the man again?* I grabbed a steel candle holder and crept towards the door slowly.

"Um... wh-who is it?" I stuttered, gripping the candle holder until my knuckles turned white.

"Open the door," the voice commanded, and my heart dropped.

Slowly unlocking the door, I opened it with a sudden quickness and swung at the horrifying man, but it was caught mid-air. Dammit! I knew I should have learned softball.

I looked up, and my eyes nearly left my head.

"A-alpha, I'm so sorry," I muttered, bowing my head and letting go of the candle holder.

"I'll let that slide, considering what you just witnessed." Alpha Mason stated, setting the candle holder atop the small dresser next to the doorway. I tried not to look up at him as he continued to talk, "I came to ask that you not mention to anyone about what you saw. The threat has been taken care of."

I nodded, not asking questions as I accidentally glanced at his bloody knuckles and shirt. "Yeah, no problemo." I nervously gave him a thumbs up, finally lifting my head to allow my lips to smile anxiously.

He looked at me weirdly before turning on his heels and retreating down the hall where he mysteriously popped up from.

I closed the door, putting my back against it and let out a deep breath I didn't know I was holding. "Stupid!" I scolded myself.

CHAPTER FOUR

◆−◇−◆

Scarlett

Sleep is superior and practically my favorite thing to do, but I was sleeping oh so peacefully when a blaring noise startled me, causing my eyes to snap wide open. I quickly moved my hand up, slamming the snooze button on the alarm multiple times. After it wouldn't shut up, I grabbed it and chucked it across the room, hearing it shatter. Much better, I hummed, snuggling into my bed's comforter.

The smell of bacon hit my nose, and my stomach grumbled like a volcano. When did mom buy *bacon*?

Wait.

I gasped, jolting up, realizing I wasn't at home. Not only was I at the alpha's mansion on community service, I'd just broken the alarm too.

I'm also five minutes late.

I jumped out of bed, rushing to the dresser. I tugged a drawer open, pulling on some clothes and tying my hair into a messy bun. At that moment, there was a knock at my door, and my eyes widened.

"Come in!" I called, digging around for my sneakers.

"Good morning, Scarlett. How'd you sleep?" Elizabeth asked, and I managed a shrug as I hopped around, trying to put my foot into my shoe.

"Decently, I guess."

She nodded and held out an ugly orange ugly vest.

You've got to be kidding me.

"Put this on over your shirt. You're working outside today."

I looked at it and cautiously grabbed it as if it would burn me. Who knows? Maybe it would.

"Do I have to wear it?" I asked. "It's embarrassing enough as it is to be doing community service,"

"Unless you want to be bothered by people or not recognized and thrown in pack cells for being mistaken as an escapee, then you don't have to," She said with a small grin.

"Noted," I mumbled, quickly pulling it over my shirt.

She smirked, "On another note, breakfast is ready. Follow me."

I nodded, thinking of the delicious food they had, because let's face it, dinner last night was terrific. Grabbing my hat, I pulled it on and followed Elizabeth out the door. Today should be *so much* fun.

As we walked downstairs, I noticed some guys were there, too.

"What up, fine thing?" I heard one of the guys say, making me stop in my tracks. I turned around and looked at him like he was insane.

"Was he talking to me?" I looked at Elizabeth for confirmation, but she was too busy trying to contain her laughter. I watched as the boys walked off, smirking over their shoulders.

"Yes, dear, he was." She started for the dining room once more, and I shook my head, following closely behind.

The audacity of the men here, I grumbled inwardly, folding my arms.

When I walked into the dining room, I found it to be silent unlike last night; but it wasn't until I realized that the Alpha and Beta were sitting at one of the dining tables talking, that I understood why.

Elizabeth leaned in and whispered, "Just get your food and eat quickly. I'll join you and then show you where you're working today."

We proceeded to a part of the dining room where all the food was served buffet style. I grabbed a biscuit, some bacon, and then snagged a small bowl of fruit. We then walked to a table towards the back, our breakfast in hand, and sat down to eat.

"Shoot," I sighed, annoyed when I realized I didn't grab a drink. The whole room was awkward for me, so you couldn't exactly blame me for trying to be as quick and inconspicuous as possible. Standing up, I headed back towards the table, grabbing a water bottle, and went to turn around to continue my path when suddenly I bumped into something, or should I say, someone.

I cautiously looked up. "Alpha Mason," I murmured, bowing my head in respect, and he gave a deep nod back.

"Scarlett, glad to see you're not stealing any more bread." He joked.

My eyes widened. Did the Alpha of War just joke with me? *A terrible joke if you ask me.*

"Funny," I replied sarcastically, making everyone around us gasp at my response back to him.

What'd I do wrong now?

"Very," He said with an amused expression, brushing past me and heading back towards his seat.

Whispers broke out as I sat back in my seat, and I could practically feel people's eyes gluing themselves to every inch of my body.

"What is all the whispering about?" I leaned over the table to ask Elizabeth. She just shrugged back.

"Probably because every person that talks to Alpha Mason never looks him in the eyes when they speak to him unless told to do so. It's his rule. He sees it as a sign of submission, so when you do look in his eyes, he takes that as disrespect. He is the Alpha of War for a reason," She pointed out.

I threw my hands down against the table lightly, rattling the salt and pepper shakers. "Why didn't he get mad at me then?" I hurriedly asked, and she shrugged once more.

"Maybe since you're just here for community service? He knows you don't know the rules around here."

"Hopefully." The last thing I needed was a mad Alpha on my hands.

***

"So, basically, you're just going to pick up any trash you see. After you're done with this area, go to the garden, and the maids will tell you what they need help with." Elizabeth pointed to the grassy area of one part of the pack that seemed to be the breeding ground or migration point for litter. I nodded and looked around some more, feeling my disgust rising the more I pointed out pieces of trash here and there. Did people seriously not know how to pick up after themselves?

Elizabeth gave me one last nod before she stalked off. I watched her go before taking a deep breath, smiling at nothing in particular other than my latex covered hands and the giant glob of garbage that was a good two feet away from my shoes and got to work.

I had this stick picker upper thingy—who knows what it's called— and I started using it to pick up trash and stick it in my trash bag. The sun was beating down on me, and I could feel sweat forming on the back of my neck. It reminded me of when I had to work with some farmers in the sectors before I got my cleaning job. After a while, my area was clear, and I tied the bag up and walked it to a bin, tossing it in.

"You just put that in the recycling bin." I heard and immediately froze, recognizing the voice.

I looked up and grabbed my hat, pulling it down, embarrassed. What was this? Who was after me like this? Karma? What did I do to deserve this, for real?

His soft chuckle made me perk up. I looked up at him, and his amused eyes met mine. What happened to the cold-hearted man I met yesterday?

"I'm starting to think you're following me around, Alpha," I accused, but Alpha Mason just laughed in response.

"Tempting, but no. I was coming from training and saw you dump trash into the bin and thought I'd be nice enough to embarrass you," He grinned.

I rolled my eyes and grabbed the bag I accidentally tossed into the recycling bin and put it into the correct container. As I looked around, I noticed a lot of people were scattered everywhere.

"If I may ask, what's up with everyone cleaning and being so jumpy today?" I asked, still looking around.

"You didn't hear?" He questioned, and I shook my head. "Everyone's getting the pack ready." He replied as if it were obvious.

"Ready for what?"

"Alpha Christian is coming to visit the pack," He answered.

My hands tightened around the trash stick, and I brought it close to my chest in surprise and maybe even a little fear. "As in like, King Christian, like Royal Alpha King Christian?" I nearly whispered.

Alpha Mason laughed at my lack of conversational skills and exasperation, nodding down at me with a big, blinding smile of amusement. "Yeah, that one."

I bit at the inside of my cheek and studied the Alpha in front of me—what a weird new thing I have been doing recently—and asked him, "Why are you not nervous, Alpha?" My hands were clammy just thinking about the King.

"Us alphas know each other well. He may be a king, but he is an Alpha and a leader of a pack just like us," He explained, and I nodded in thought.

Duh, Scarlett.

"You should probably go help the other maids," He added a beat later.

I gave him a deep nod of my head to show respect and turned, slowly walking to the garden.

Alpha Christian was coming? When? Why?

***

After a long day of tedious work, I happily went back to my room and slumped against my temporary bed, glad to sit for once. As I sat taking off my shoes, I realized that the odd funk I had been smelling all the way back to my room was me. The smell of trash, dirt, and who knows what else obviously followed me all the back to my room like the perfume of a haughty old lady. Is this what it means to be a criminal?

Shaking my head at my inner thoughts, I pulled myself up and went to use all the hot water in my shower—you know because I had to get something out of this other than a lesson learned because who knew how long it had been since I'd taken a shower for more than ten minutes.

Stepping out with a towel tightly wrapped around my body, I quickly changed and used it to dry my hair, tossing it into my hamper afterward.

When I plopped back down onto my bed, I glanced at my new alarm clock—Thanks, Elizabeth—and saw that it was ten till dinner was ready; so I thought I'd just go ahead and head down towards the main hall since I had nothing else to do.

As I trudged towards the dining room, I noticed that no one was about. Nevertheless, I continued making my way through the mansion, but then quickly realized that it was dead silent.

"What are you doing?" someone hissed.

I pivoted on my heel just to see Elizabeth rushing towards me. I cocked a brow and frowned, slightly confused by her weird behavior. I tilted my head questioningly as she got right up to me, her fingers grabbing at my wrists like our lives depended on it. I opened my mouth, bewildered, "I was heading towards the dining hall for dinner?"

"Are you crazy? Everyone knows that dinner is being served in their rooms tonight! Do you ever read the notes left on your desk? The King is here!" She hurried out and my eyes widened in shock.

"He came today?!"

Elizabeth nodded, pushing me towards the stairs and shushing me, but I stopped abruptly when a scent hit my nose. The smell was so strong, so poignant that my wolf started stirring within me. *It smelled amazing.*

"That smell..." I mumbled, but she cocked an eyebrow like she was confused.

"What are you talking about, Scarlett?! Get to your room! No one is allowed in the halls when the King is here!" She tried rushing me.

"Then, why are you here?" I interrogated her, folding my arms stubbornly.

"To save your ass!"

Good point.

I hurried towards the stairs and was about to run up them when Elizabeth grabbed my arms. "What are you-" I was cut off by a low growl.

My stomach dropped as I turned and looked up the staircase to see Mason and another man descending, the scent from earlier hitting me stronger than before. I took a deep breath, relishing in it, feeling my wolf coming alive. It was when I made eye contact with the mysterious man that my wolf nearly howled in excitement. His eyes were like pools of gold shining brightly at me as he stared me down.

"Mate," We said in unison.

"Holy hell," Elizabeth breathed as the man started to make his way towards me.

When he came closer, less than a meter from where I stood, I noted his tallness. He was taller than me, a whole foot perhaps, and I had to angle my head up just to maintain eye contact. I felt like an ant as he stared down at me.

"Your name?" His voice was husky, the sound of it sweeping over me like a spring breeze.

"S-Scarlett," I stuttered.

A low growl emitted from his chest as my sight became fuzzy, and my thoughts became a jumbled mess.

"Call me Christian," were the last words I heard him speak before the world shifted, and everything started falling and darkening until it went completely black.

CHAPTER FIVE

───◆◇◆───

Scarlett

I groaned as my head pounded. My eyes fluttered open, and I looked over to see a worried-looking Elizabeth.

"I had the weirdest dream," I croaked out, and she pursed her lips, her eyebrows raising to her hairline. "I was mated..." I paused, the thought almost too outrageous to even utter, "to the king." My voice was a whisper, and the headache that was slowly forming into a migraine wasn't helping matters. I was so afraid that someone would hear me, but she looked at me like I had just told her the funniest thing.

She opened her mouth to speak, and I thought she was going to tell me something along the lines of 'How crazy, Scarlett! You and the King!?' Instead, she only said, "The King, you say?" I nodded and closed my eyes for a second.

When I finally opened them, I noticed where I was. "Wait. Why am I here?" I looked at Elizabeth frantically.

"You fainted," a voice said, startling me. I grabbed at my chest, not liking the feeling the voice sent running down my spine and loving it at the same time.

Ignoring the delightful shivers, I dropped my hand and looked towards the doorway. "You've got to be kidding me," I mumbled, noticing the small smirk that danced across the king's lips as he saw my state of shock.

"King Christian," I spoke courteously, trying to sit up to show my respect—because my mother would have slapped me with her chancla if I did otherwise—but he quickly made his way to my side to help me sit up, to my utter confusion, and as soon as he touched me, sparks traipsed down my arm. So, it wasn't a dream? Now I felt incredibly embarrassed and a little excited, too.

Mates.

I, Scarlett Rose Madison, am mates with the king! This had to be a dream. Having a mate was the one thing every wolf looked forward to when they became of age. The rumor is that the Moon Goddess, the deity we wolves' worship, crafted the mate bond to make our perfect match. She did this so none of her creations would be lonely. You were matched from birth, and in this case, I was born to be mated to a king.

"Please, call me Christian." His husky voice floated through my ears, calming me instantly. His scent was almost overpowering, but I couldn't get enough of it. *He indeed was my mate.*

Elizabeth stood up. "I'll give you guys some privacy," she smiled, her face bright and hands clasped behind her back as she walked out.

As soon as Elizabeth was out of the room, and the two of us sat alone, he looked at me with concerned eyes. "How are you feeling?" he asked, making my wolf croon at his concern for us.

Woah there, girl.

"I'm okay. Just a little shocked, I guess."

He nodded in understanding and pulled a chair next to the bed. "I get that." His sudden proximity made my wolf spring to life, making me feel all awkward as I looked everywhere but him.

"Well," he shifted uncomfortably in his seat—probably because his mate was acting like a freak around him—and cleared his throat, continuing, "tomorrow you'll be coming back to my pack with me."

While my wolf howled in happiness that she would be with her mate, I felt my mouth drop open in shock. I felt my whole body physically dropping as I curled in on myself in horror. Go to the Royal Pack? With him? *Tomorrow?*

"Wait. What?" I couldn't leave with him. I barely even knew him!

"You're my mate, what did you expect? I'm the king and the Alpha of the Royals. I can't leave them without an Alpha for too long." He sounded slightly amused, but I shook my head at him, not finding the slightest humor in the situation.

"I have family around here. You can't just take me away from them. Plus, I haven't even finished my community service yet. You also have to consider that I barely know you. No offense, your majes— I mean, Christian, but it just doesn't feel right to just up and leave with you tomorrow..." I trailed off, a little breathless.

To my surprise, he nodded in understanding. He seemed to be deep in thought for a moment like he was contemplating something vital. Well, I mean, the fate of his mate should be important, right? He then looked back up to meet my intense gaze with his calm and collected one.

"What if I took care of your community service?" I felt my shoulders relaxing at the thought of no more sweaty trash-collecting as he continued, "As for your family, they can come and see you whenever you'd like. I would let them join the pack, but as you know, you have to be born into it or mated to someone within." I tensed up again and raised a finger to him, to stop him in his tracks, but he beat me to the punch, "And as for the hesitancy to leave with me, I understand. I'm not going to pressure you into something you do not want to do, but please consider that since our wolves have met, the bond has already started. They'll yearn for one another, and you'll go into heat very soon." He finished.

I instantly dropped my trembling hand to my lap, the nerves taking over again. Heat was something every female wolf went through after meeting their mate. It was there to urge the mating process along, and until you mated with your other half, you'd continue to have it. The pain a female wolf felt during heat was unbearable without your mate by your side. I always dreaded the day mine would come— or at least I did before I stopped believing in the whole soulmate thing. From the very moment my mother sat me down and explained the mating process to me, it was something I never really wanted to go through. Terrible conversation to have over dinner, believe me.

Inhaling to calm myself, I looked over at Alpha Christian with my fierce eyes. "I just met you. Before I met you, I didn't even think mates existed. Mates were just a fairy-tale, a feel-good story for little girls to cling to and dream about." I said the last part quietly, noticing the small rumble of a growl in his chest.

It was true, though. My sister thrived on the hope that someday she would find her mate, but I never cared much for it. My mother tried to explain the kaleidoscope of feelings one gets when finding their mate, the number of incredible sensations you get, but I couldn't believe her. How could I, when all I'd ever known, was the struggle and pain of being born into the Sectors? How could there ever be any good in the world when there was stuff like that? It seemed like a myth and having my mother and father, no matter how much they believed in mates, never getting the chance to find theirs didn't help. I never had any tangible proof to make me believe it. My mother would tell us hundreds of stories about them, but I didn't pay a lick of attention to most of it.

"I can't leave my family how they are. I can't let them suffer while I go off to some happily ever after. I just can't, I'm sorry." I looked up at him, and he tilted his head to the side in confusion.

"We live in the sectors." I clarified, worried about his reaction, yet he looked deep in thought for a moment.

"I'll get them into the Power Pack. It's the closest one to ours."

My heart picked up speed. *That's Alpha Ryker's pack.* No way.

"Really?"

"You're my mate, Scarlett. Your wish is my command." He gave me a small, cheesy smile, and I couldn't help but notice how my name rolled off his tongue with ease. It couldn't have sounded better from anyone else.

This seems so surreal.

"You're going to be the Luna and the Queen of the royals. I'd rather you be happy knowing your family is in good hands and be able to lead with me without the constant need for worry," he articulated, "Everyone starts somewhere in a relationship. We just have to try first. You'll have your own room, we'll take it slow, but please come back with me. I cannot fathom you here alone, I will worry too much."

I thought about it, and reluctantly nodded. "Okay."

"But," his expression furrowed, and he looked distraught.

"What's wrong?" I asked immediately, and he sighed, pinching the bridge of his nose.

"There's something I need to tell you," I nodded for him to continue, but couldn't help but feel uneasy. He looked back up at me and started. "My father was pressuring me into finding a queen, and if I didn't find one in the time I was given, he was going to find one for me. He's arranged a mating for me."

Oh, Goddess.

"And?" I pressed.

"And he did, but don't worry though. When we get home, I will show you off and tell everyone you're my mate, the one true queen, and that you're the only one I want. She isn't taking your place. I haven't even spoken a word to the girl. The coronation was months away, but now it's not going to happen. I just wanted you to know that. I don't want to start this relationship off with lies."

I nodded, respecting his honesty. "Okay." Maybe this wouldn't be so bad.

As I sat and pondered on the whole situation, I realized just how the fate of mates works. They say fate does things to make your paths cross, and I'm living proof that it does—that damn bread.

I didn't believe it at first. I believed in love, but mates? A soulmate at that? I now knew that it was no lie considering the way his mere presence affected me. His smell alone drove me crazy, and his touch sent chills down my spine.

Though, as I watched people pack my room up and take my belongings to the sleek, black car Christian had arrived in, I saw how real this all was. Hours ago, I was doing my community service for stealing bread, and now I was on the path to standing beside Christian as Queen. How's that for a change of plans?

As I sat nervously in the back of his car, my heart pounded rapidly in my chest. First stop: my house to notify my parents about this new *arrangement* and grab some of my belongings. They'd either freak or be happy— probably both. I smiled, thinking about them finding out they were going to be in a pack and no longer in the sectors. I was a lucky girl, that's for sure, but the future was kind of daunting.

After a while, I let out a yawn and laid my head against the window.

"Tired?" Christian asked, and I nodded.

"Very. It turns out that community service is exhausting." I joked, and his soft chuckle followed, the deep vocals relaxing me.

"Mason told me you didn't do much," he teased, and I let out a gasping scoff.

"That... now that is..." I looked away, thinking about it, "is actually very true."

People in packs can learn to pick up their own trash.

Christian let out a laugh, shaking his head. "At least you attended."

I frowned, looking over at him. "Thank you for helping me get out of it, Christian, but to be honest... I don't think I took this as seriously because after living in the sectors and having to fight every day to stay alive, cleaning up trash after people who have everything that I don't is a slap in the face. I mean, Goddess, people can't even pick up their own trash! That's the issue you all have in packs? To find people who will clean up your trash? How about us in the sectors? We fight to find someone to help us when we're sick or dying." I muttered, and he looked away from my stare.

"I'm sorry, I never saw it that way," he mumbled.

"How could you? You never had to live a life like that. I'm not bashing you, because it was your elders who banished us to the Personal Status

System and not you, but sometimes you have to think about others, even if they're below you and might not seem that important."

Christian went silent, and I sighed, thinking I'd gone too far. I need to learn when to keep my mouth shut.

"I'm willing to learn," he blurted out, and my head snapped to look at him as my eyes widened in shock.

"What?"

"I'm willing to learn and listen. I want to know what it was like for you. I want to know how my people are being treated in the sectors. I do feel terrible for them, Scarlett. I have tried for years to find a way to make it better, so maybe with your help we can work on that."

I stared at him with my mouth slightly agape. "For starters, you can end them and put your people in real packs." He shook his head with a look of sorrow.

"It's not that easy. It's a very long process that I have been fighting to get passed for years, believe it or not."

I looked his face over for any signs of a lie, but there were none. After a minute, I finally spoke, "You truly have thought about this and have been working on a plan to end the Sectors?"

"Cross my heart, Scarlett."

I looked away from him and out the window as I watched the scenery go by. "Then I'm more than happy to tell you everything about the Sectors and help you find a better way of living for my people, but not tonight. Tonight, I want to focus on my family."

"Understood. Are we okay?"

I looked over at him and couldn't help but let out a small laugh. "We've known each other for a day, and you already think we're in a fight?"

He cracked a small smile. "Honestly, I just don't want to get off on the wrong foot here. As you said, we've only known each other for a day."

"We'll make it work," I half-smiled. "It's just going to take time for us to learn each other's worlds."

"Agreed, so do you think your parents are going to hate me then?"

I shrugged. "Who knows when it comes to them two."

"That's very helpful, thank you."

I belched out a laugh, shaking my head. "I'm just saying... I don't know how they will feel. We have different views, and we don't talk about the system much."

"Well, now I'm nervous, and I'm the King... how wonderful."

I bit the inside of my cheek to hold back a smirk. He can shake in his boots for one night.

"Well," I smiled, "if it makes you feel any better, my sister will probably freak when she sees you."

He raised a brow. "Is that so?"

"Oh, I'm sure. She thinks you're total eye candy."

He chuckled and asked, "Well, you don't seem too fond of her."

I scoffed and shrugged. "She's a brat, but she's my little sister, so I have to love her."

He chuckled at my response, and soon enough, we came to the familiar house I grew up in.

"Are you ready for all this, *King Christian?*" I winked, and he rolled his eyes.

"You make it sound like they're about to eat me alive."

"Maybe... who knows." I grinned, hopping out of the car.

He was quick to catch up with me as I approached the front door. I turned to face him after I started to feel the nerves kick in, too.

"How about I go in first? You can stand at the door."

"As you wish."

When I walked through the small house, I heard the clinking of pans and followed the sounds into the kitchen. "Mom," I smiled, walking in just as she started cooking. She jumped a mile into the air and turned around to look at me with a startled expression. I laughed at her disgruntled state, her wide eyes, crazy messy bun, and flour-stained apron.

"¡Dios mío! Why are you home? Did you steal something else?!" She accused, pointing her wooden spoon at me and approaching me with a fiery gaze.

"No, mom!" I protested as she came closer to me, my hands going up to shield my most prized asset, my face, from her wrath, but I had a sinking feeling that she was going to take a shoe off any second and beat me with it.

"Mom! I didn't do anything! Calm down!"

I heard a soft chuckle from Christian, but she didn't hear it. How could she not feel the power radiating off him? Did the rage for her favorite daughter blind her senses?

"Then why are you home?"

"Geesh, it's nice to see you too!" She rolled her eyes, walking back to the stove to continue cooking. "Where's dad?" I asked.

"Stop beating around the bush, what did you do?" she interrogated, whipping back around to glare at me once more.

Here goes nothing, "I... met my mate." I slowly revealed.

Right after those words left my mouth, the spoon completely dropped from her hands. "What! What do you mean you met him? Are you playing games with me?!"

"I met him, mom. I really did find him," I repeated, and her face lit up—all anger leaving her.

"Oh, my goodness! That's amazing, sweetie! Who is it? Is he cute?"

"I know and you— well, you actually know him, and yes he's very cute." I could practically see his smirk from behind me.

"Wait, is he here? I knew I smelled a new scent! I thought you just picked it up from The War Pack." she gushed as she walked forward, but before she could get any farther, I stepped in front of her, stopping her in her tracks.

"Where's dad and Ashlee?" I interrupted.

"Somewhere, now move!" I was pushed aside as she walked toward the front door to see who I had brought home to her, but I grabbed her arm, causing her to look back at me.

"When you see him, please know that he is already making me happy and who he is doesn't define him," I pleaded. She gave me a concerned look and pulled her arm from my grasp and left my sight as she rounded a corner. "Oh, Goddess," I muttered, placing my hands onto my face.

I heard a shriek, not even half a second later. As soon as she rounded the corner and came into view, I immediately noticed her taking off her flip flop in her frenzied wake, and I threw my arms in front of myself to protect me from her craziness.

"Madre!" I screeched as she continually whacked me with it.

"You could have told me it was *the king* so that I could have cleaned up a bit! I didn't know it would be him!" she yelled, still in shock, and still whacking me in between every other word.

Christian appeared around the corner with an amused look. I glared at him through my attack.

"Save me," I mouthed, inching my way over to him as my mother backed up towards the wall adjacent to him. He laughed at this horrid display of abuse, pulling me into his side. "Save me from... *the flip flop*," I pleaded dramatically from under his arm, my hands going up to clutch at his shirt. He stared down at me with an award-winning smile. As I kept staring into his bright eyes, watching as they shimmered in and out of that golden hue, I knew he felt it, too— that tug.

We were so close, too close, and I wasn't the only one feeling it. The feeling of being in an almost-embrace with him was making me feel some type of way, but I wrangled in those feelings to focus on my crazed mother. I moved away slightly, but he kept his arm around my waist. These feelings were mutual, but I chose not to acknowledge them right now. I could ask him about it later because he undoubtedly knew more about this bonding thing than I did.

With my eyes back on my mother, I watched as she started darting around the kitchen. I couldn't help but be amused at the sight. The house wasn't even dirty, but she was such a clean freak. I don't think she's fully comprehending this.

I was brought out of my thoughts when Christian subconsciously tightened his hold around my waist. My body instantly leaned into his touch, and I glanced at him, only to see him still staring at me, his eyes full of gold now. The bond was strengthening already.

"Y-you're mated to... the king? You? To the king?"

I turned away from Christian so fast when my mom started talking to us; I swear I got whiplash. As she came and took in our appearance, her face warped into one of complete and utter bewilderment. I didn't know whether to be offended or not.

"You are, aren't you? Oh, my goddess, you are. It's so obvious." Then I heard her mutter things in Spanish, causing me to snicker.

"I didn't know you had a background like that," He leaned down and whispered into my ear as my mother turned to face the stove, trying to compose herself while I, on the other hand, seemed to be losing composure with the feelings he stirred inside me. My wolf was relishing in the attention.

Doing what I do best, I tried to ignore these strange feelings and told him, "I don't know a lot of Spanish since I was born here, just like my dad. He's American, but my mom is from Mexico and is the only one who speaks Spanish most of the time." He nodded in interest, taking in the information.

"Your father is going to have a heart attack." Mom said, breaking free from her thoughts.

"Oh, I'm sure he will." I mused and was about to say something else when a loud voice made my eyes widen.

"What the hell?" was heard throughout the kitchen. Christian pulled me impossibly closer to him, so close I could feel the ridges beneath his shirt as he turned on high alert, just until I realized it was my brat of a sister.

"Language!" My mom scolded, but Ashlee ignored her like a true Madison, taking in Christian's appearance.

"Y-you're... you're k-king—"

"Are you going to get that sentence out yet or...?" I mocked, and she squinted her eyes at me, her cheeks reddening.

"Why is he here?" she whispered to me like he wasn't right there.

"He's her mate," my mom stated, turning to look back at us, her lips pulled up into a wide smile. I couldn't tell if she was okay with the situation or upset. "Well... formally introduce us." Mom encouraged me.

"Right. Christian, this is my mom, Selene, and my sister, Ashlee. Mom, Ash, this is Christian."

He held his hand out for each of them to shake and they did, so starstruck, it was amusing.

"*Wow.* You're hotter in person." The words bluntly left my sister's mouth, and without a second thought, a growl ripped through me, surprising everyone in the room, including myself. I quickly covered my mouth in embarrassment, and Christian grinned at me, enjoying my possessiveness.

Stupid wolf.

"Aw! My sweet baby is growing up," Mom cried out, pulling me to her. This was so embarrassing!

"Oh, I have got to show you baby pictures of Scarlett!" Ashlee exclaimed to Christian, who smirked at my wide-eyed stare and shaking head.

"I'd love to see them."

I stared after him in horror. "No!" I called out as she took him to the living room to grab the album. I went to go after him, but my mother tugged me back.

"Ah, muy guapo?" Mom asked, and I let out a soft laugh.

"Yes, mom. He's very handsome."

She grinned at me.

"You're not mad?" I asked.

"Mad? Why would I be mad, Scarlett?"

I shrugged nonchalantly. "I just know your distaste for The Royals, the system, and everything," I mumbled, and she laid a loving hand on my cheek.

"Scarlett, I'm not mad. I would never be mad at you for finding your mate. This is good for you! You can't blame him for something his elders caused a long time ago. I'm happy for you, sweetie."

What a relief.

"I have to tell you something." she nodded, and I took a breath. "I'm leaving tonight."

Her eyes widened, and she ran a weathered hand through her tied-back hair. "What? His pack is almost ten hours away!" I nodded with a soft smile.

"He agreed to move you." her eyes widened at my news.

"W-what are you saying, Scarlett?" Her shocked face made me smile even more.

"Mom, he's relocating you guys for me! You'll live in the Power Pack! Just an hour away from me." I beamed, and she let out a happy sob, throwing her arms around me.

"Thank the Goddess," she sobbed out.

"Happy tears, I hope."

"Of course, Scarlett." I gave her a teary smile at her response and looked over, seeing Christian laughing at the photos of me.

"Your dad is down in the mines today. I'm upset he won't get to see you off."

He probably wouldn't have cared much anyway, I thought to myself.

"That's okay. You guys weren't going to see me for another week or two anyway. Let's surprise him. I know dad works so hard around here, mom, and I know he and I didn't leave on good terms, so tell him for me, will you? When he's not so tired and in a good mood? Tell him things are going to be looking up from here on out, yeah? I'll tell him everything once we meet at the Power Pack, okay?" She thought about it and nodded.

"I'll inform Ashlee. Thank you so much, sweetie,"

I looked to Christian. "Don't thank me, thank him."

***

"It's getting late, we better head out," Christian said to me as we all sat in the living room, talking after eating the dinner my mom had prepared for us. I almost felt bad for eating the dinner that I know she worked hard to make for her, my father, and sister, knowing there wasn't much for them to begin with.

"I agree," I half smiled, but deep down, I was growing nervous. This was a big step for me. Moving in with a guy? King Alpha Christian at that? I had been very much prepared to live and die in the sectors, so this was an entirely new and different path I was not expecting to go down. I hadn't even known it was a path I could have potentially taken, that my destiny had been leading me this way ever since I was born.

Minutes later, we were saying our goodbyes.

"Bye, Scarlett, I love you." Mom said, and I smiled, pulling away from our embrace. After we all said our bittersweet goodbyes, I headed towards Christian's car and my new life.

"Ready?" he asked, opening the door for me.

"Ready as I'll ever be."

CHAPTER SIX

◆◇◆

Scarlett

I stood in awe at the palace before me. I never thought I'd get a chance to see it, and in person at that. It was beautiful. Every inch of the place was detailed in such an elegant manner. I felt so out of place. I glanced down at my simple tank top, jeans, and sneakers and then glanced at Christian, who was grabbing our bags. His expensively tailored suit clung well to his muscular frame, but most importantly, he looked like he belonged.

How did I get a chance to be with him? Deep down, questions of fate and destiny started to kindle to life, and I couldn't stop that one burning question from igniting inside of my head.

Why me?

He could have been mated to a gorgeous woman, someone from the War Pack, or even the Intelligence pack! Instead, he got me: Plain Jane and a simpleton.

"I can help," I mumbled, my sudden inner turmoil spilling into my voice as I walked towards him.

"No, thank you. I've got it." I reluctantly nodded and trailed behind him up the stairs to the main entrance.

Once we entered the pack, it took us almost an hour to get to where the palace was. Houses were scattered here and there, and they weren't precisely small ones either. The Royal Pack wouldn't have seemed like a big pack since you had to be born into it or mated to someone from it, but over the hundreds of years it had been alive, it had grown. People found mates outside of the pack, moved with their mate back to the pack and got married, had children, and so forth. It just kept happening, and from what I'd heard around the sectors, it seemed like a lot of servants and maids lived throughout the palace and some homes around the area, too, probably some guards as well, if I had to guess.

As we climbed the last of the stairs to the palace, a couple of guards opened the door for us, muttering a 'your majesty,' as a butler came to grab our bags and dashed away after Christian notified him to put them in his room.

I watched as people stood around, curiously looking at me, probably wondering what a girl like me was doing with their king. As if noticing my uneasiness, Christian put a reassuring hand on the small of my back.

"How about I take you to my room, and you can rest? I need to speak with my father." I nodded as we heard a small gasp at the mention of Christian's room. Glancing over, a woman stood whispering to the people around her.

"Who is she?" I heard faintly as Christian and I started walking towards the stairs next to them.

"No telling. She's probably a stray he took pity on. I wonder how Amanda will feel?" a voice joked.

Christian came to a halt, and I instantly knew he had heard the last one.

"Enough! If I hear any more negative comments, I won't be afraid to banish you from the pack. You're a royal, so act like one." he snapped as their eyes widened in fear.

"Come on, Scarlett," Christian grumbled, pulling me to him as we continued walking once more. Going up the stairs, I could practically feel the stare of everyone as shock settled over them. On the outside, I contained my utter excitement, but my wolf was howling with joy.

He stood up for us.

Feeling giddy the whole way up the staircase, we made it to the very top floor. Once at the top, I saw a keypad next to the knob, making me realize that you had to have a code to even get into the hallway. After he typed the code in, Christian opened the door and guided us towards yet another door. For a second time, he typed in a code. This place seems safe. Excessively safe, I thought.

However, after stepping through the threshold and into his room, I was full of amazement. It was like a huge penthouse!

"Wow, quite the bachelor's pad you have here," I joked, sidestepping Christian as he shrugged off his blazer. His soft chuckle floated through the pristine air of his room— no, his own apartment— as I took in the elegant floor plan. There was a beautiful sized kitchen and living room that hit you right as you walked in. Other doors were around, leading to who knows where. I did a full spin to catch a glimpse of every inch but stopped right as he started speaking.

"Oh yes, the ladies just love it." I chuckled lightly at his joke, but deep down, I felt my chest tighten, wondering how many girls he had been with, while I'd barely left the sectors. I ignored the intrusive thoughts, though, in favor of listening to Christian's baritone drawl. "I'll give you a tour later, but for now I can show you my room so that you can rest."

He grabbed our bags once more and was about to take me to his room when he suddenly stopped. Dropping the bags again, he turned and asked with the cutest raise of an eyebrow, "Unless you want your room right away? It's just not made up fully yet."

"That's very considerate of you, but for a quick rest, your room will be fine, if that's okay with you? Tonight, I can sleep in the guest room. I just don't want to rush things." I replied, fiddling with my thumbs.

"What's mine is yours, and, of course, I understand. Please, tell me if I'm ever overstepping the mark. Mates are different for males. We tend to want to be around our other half twenty-four seven. It's more of a possessive protection thing than anything else."

I smiled, giving him a slight nod.

He beamed at my smile, making my heart melt just a little, and told me to follow him. I obediently walked after him and followed him into his room. As soon as he pushed open the smooth wood of his door, I was flooded with amazement for the second time in a span of five minutes.

The bedroom was big and roomy. It had a huge flat screen tv on the wall in front of a king-sized bed that looked oh-so-comfortable. A door was open, and you could tell it led to a huge master bathroom. The dark color schemes of the room set a grave mood. It was like nothing I'd ever seen before.

"Your room is very nice," I said, and he smirked.

"Why, thank you."

We grinned at each other as I grabbed my suitcase from his hand, our fingers brushing ever so gently, causing my wolf to stir with delight at the sudden contact and the tingly sensations that shot beneath my skin. *Calm down, calm down, calm down*!

"Uh... do you mind if I take a quick shower?" I asked, mostly trying to steer my mind towards something else.

Christian, dropping his suitcase on his bed, walked over and warmly cupped my face between his large hands with an amused expression. The tingles started again, and this time the prolonged contact was making me feel things a hundred times more.

"What did I say literally two minutes ago? What's mine is yours. You don't have to ask me. Feel free to shower, rest, watch tv; I don't care. Do what you please. I'll be back up shortly." He leaned down, laying a soft kiss on my forehead that caused butterflies to burst free within my stomach.

"Thank you," I whispered as he pulled away.

"I'll see you in a few."

I gave him a thumbs-up, watching his retreating figure as he closed the bedroom door behind him. Taking in a deep breath, I dropped my suitcase and let out a small squeal. I've known him for a whole two days, and I was already falling for him. No matter how cringe worthy I sounded, it was true. Was that crazy?

I opened my suitcase, grabbing some necessities and clothes, and headed into the bathroom. Making sure I locked the door; I set my things down on the counters and immediately set my eyes on the walk-in shower.

Christian

I left the room, hoping Scarlett would be able to rest. Our journey from the sectors was long, and I could see how exhausted she was. Once out in the hallway, I had to take a moment to compose myself before I went to speak with my father. I didn't know what I was going to say, but I knew I had to tell him and demand that my coronation with Amanda be called off.

I would not take another woman as my queen when my true mate, the true queen, was resting in my bedroom, just a few feet away from me. It seemed so unreal; I had almost given up hope on finding my mate.

Though, fate works in mysterious ways and here I was… In the same place as her, and already completely smitten with that fiery red head who never left my mind. I shook my head, leaving my thoughts, and headed to my office where my father waited.

As I reached for the doorknob, my heart picked up its pace. Conversations with my father never went too well— they always ended up in an argument. I prayed to the Goddess today would be different.

"It's about time, I've been waiting for twenty minutes." he grumbled, shifting in his chair.

"Sorry, I had someone to tend to before I came," I walked over, taking a seat behind my desk.

"I hope that someone is Amanda?" he raised a brow.

"No, father, it's not. I need to tell you something very important."

"If you're trying to meddle with my plans for you and Amanda, forget about it. It's final, you need a queen, Christian. I gave you plenty of opportunities to look for one yourself, but you never did. I had no choice but to do it myself."

"Because a small part of me had to have hope that I would find my mate, just like you did." I shot back.

"And where did that get you? Nowhere. It's rare to find your mate, Christian, you know this. I'm sorry, but I'm not changing my decision unless your mate walks through that door right now."

"She doesn't have to because she's currently resting in my room." I stated, trying not to smile as his eyes widened.

"Wait, what?"

I gave him a smug look. "I found my mate. Her name is Scarlett Madison and so far, she's a great woman."

"Where did you meet her? What pack is she from?" he questioned.

"I met her at The War pack, but she's not from a pack... she's from The Sectors." I watched as he looked away, deep in thought.

"The Sectors?" he spoke barely above a whisper.

"Dad, you can't judge her just because of where she comes from. She had no control over it."

He shook his head. "That's not what I'm worried about..." he trailed off and I leaned forward.

"What is it then?"

"You cannot let the church officials find out. If the church finds out she's from the sectors, they will not accept her, and the head of the church will come down here to find you a different queen. Christian, listen to me when I say this, you tell *no one*." he emphasized.

I nodded but looked at him in confusion. "Why are the officials so against the sectors? They're the reason all this happened in the first place."

"I don't know, but I do know that fact. Trust me, you do not want to let them know."

"Ok... I won't."

"Good," he nodded. "Then I accept, we will go and tell Amanda that her coronation will no longer be happening."

My eyes widened. "You really mean that?"

His features softened as he looked back at me. "How can I keep you apart from your soulmate? You are meant to be with her, and I can't stand in the way of that."

"What about Mom?"

His expression abruptly changed. "You know how your mother is. She's on a trip right now visiting some friends, I wouldn't bother telling her until she's back and you can do it in person."

I gulped. "Are you sure I shouldn't call her now and tell her? It's rather important."

He shook his head. "No, she'll take it better in person. You better get yourself prepared for that. Your mother is not easily accepting."

I rolled my eyes at the reminder. "Don't I know it."

I was about to speak when I felt a wave of uneasiness through the mate bond.

"Dad, I'm sorry but I have to go. I'll meet with you later to tell Amanda. Something is wrong with Scarlett; I can feel it through the bond."

He waved me off. "Go to her. We have plenty of time to tell Amanda."

I nodded, relieved the conversation had gone so well. The only thing dampening my mood was the fact I had to hide that Scarlett was from The Sectors. It just felt wrong.

I left my office, hurrying down to my room to see what had gotten my mate upset.

Scarlett

After taking a shower, which felt heavenly and totally unlike the shower back at my own home, I felt refreshed and relaxed. The smell of my shampoo lingered in the misty bathroom air as I dried my hair, watching my reflection as I worked the towel through my locks. When I was done, I went back into Christian's room. My hand danced over the soft fabric of his bed as I made my way to one side of it. I slowly pulled the covers back and slipped in. His soft duvet rubbed against my legs, and his fluffy pillow felt like my head was resting upon a cloud. It was the most comfortable bed I'd ever been in, which wasn't saying much, considering I lived in the sectors and used a hard mattress to sleep.

Looking around the room, I felt content. Christian's scent was invading my head as it was attached to everything, and I took a deep breath in, savoring it all. The action brought back memories of the tales my mom used to tell me about mates and how their scents and sparks are some of the best things about it all— how your mate can instantly calm you and how protected you feel around one another. One just couldn't get enough. I remembered her telling me about— oh no.

My eyes sprung open as I realized how real this was. It was so real that it meant one thing: heat. I was going to go into heat soon. Christian even mentioned it before. How could I forget? Heat has been said to be the worst part of being a female werewolf.

I left my current fairy tale as reality sat in. I sat up straight in the bed and felt my mind start to race as I stared at the blackened screen of the TV for Goddess knows how long. I guess too long because the door opened after some time, revealing Christian.

"I could feel your uneasiness through our bond. What's wrong?" he quickly asked, walking over to me.

I groaned, covering my face in embarrassment. "We met two days ago," I started, and he nodded.

"Yes?"

I looked away from his gaze. "And we're mates."

"Yes? Where are you going with this exactly? Are you worried about us being mates?" he asked with amusement in his voice, yet with a slight edge to it.

"No, it's just that, uh. You know..." I trailed off, but he still looked at me in confusion.

"Know...?" he dragged on.

Oh, my Goddess.

"I'll go into heat soon!" I cried out impatiently.

His eyebrows slowly drifted up to his hairline. Then, as if suddenly getting it, "Oh." Oh? That was all he had to say. "I'll be here if that's what you're worried about?"

I shook my head. "I know you will be here. It's just that it's scary to think about that happening, Christian. When a female wolf goes into heat, it's so painful, and you feel as if your body is on fire burning you from the inside out." I confessed fearfully.

He sighed, motioning for me to move over. I did, leaning against the headboard as he sat next to me, wrapping his arm around me. He pulled me to his chest, and this feeling of safety and security settled over me, feelings I haven't really ever felt before, causing my insides to jump.

"Did your mom tell you the whole thing?" he asked, and I nodded.

"I remember parts, obviously, but as I said, I didn't believe in all that, so I really didn't listen."

"Well, it seems bad, but it's not. It won't be painful for you because I'll be here. Your mate's touch is enough to make some of the pain go away, so it won't be as bad, and I'm not going to do anything you're not ready for, Scarlett. I'll sit here and hold you all night until it passes if I have to. Your pain is my pain."

I didn't know that.

"Okay," I mumbled, snuggling up to him. He let out a small chuckle, pulling a blanket over both of us, and for the first time in a long time, I fell right asleep.

CHAPTER SEVEN

※ ◇ ※

Scarlett

That night, I stayed in the guest room. It was easy to tell that Christian wanted me to stay with him, but I just needed some time to process everything, so I rolled out of his incredibly comfortable king-sized bed and slinked my sorry butt to the guest room. Luckily, it was right across the hall, so I wasn't too far away.

That thought alone was enough to get me thinking. I always wanted to be near him, I still wanted to touch him and to be with him, and I'd only just met him!

The next morning, I woke up to an empty penthouse, if you could call it that. I walked around the large living space in a pair of comfortable shorts and a tank top, deciding to explore the kitchen. Like the rest of the place, it was open and very sleek, the appliances stainless steel and countertops a smooth marble. It all looked costly, almost too expensive compared to what my family and I were used to. Walking around the island, I opened the fridge to find something to eat, but as soon as the clean, white light of the refrigerator hit my eyes, I knew I was doomed. Of course, there was no food.

I wondered whether Christian even came here other than to sleep. He did show me his office on this floor, so maybe he was there? I opened the door to his spectacular penthouse and quietly headed down the hall. Once I came to his office, I focused my hearing on seeing if he was in a meeting. It was silent. I knocked on the door, but there was no response. Slowly opening the door, I called out, "Coming in!" but I came up to an empty office.

"Hmph," I let out, deciding just to go and look for him downstairs. I could also get some breakfast on the main floor while I was at it. Walking out of the door that led to the steps, I got a couple of feet away from the closing door before I froze. I needed to change my clothes! Spinning with the grace of a three-legged horse, I scrambled for the door before it closed completely.

"Wait!" I yelled, but to no avail. The door clicked shut, and I was left frantically tugging on the door. I didn't remember the code!

"You have got to be kidding me," I grumbled, letting my head bang against the door.

Slowly heading down the stairs to the main foyer, I finally made it to the living room and the nearby kitchen. Everyone in the room froze, their conversations dying down to shocked nothingness as they looked at me with wide eyes. Don't do it. Don't do it. Don't do it.… I smiled awkwardly and gave the room full of elegant and fancy people a stiff wave of my hand and a bow of my head. You did it, Scarlett, you really did it. I felt like running out of the room or maybe getting swallowed whole by El Cucuy. Instead, I tried focusing on Christian's scent, but too many people were around for me to catch it.

My wolf felt irritated being away from her mate, but as my stomach grumbled, I knew that right now, food was my main priority, not sedating her needy wants, and definitely not the awkward situation I had dug myself into.

"Luna!" someone called out just as I started to make my way towards the kitchen. I tensed up, raising my head to see someone walking towards me. Luna? *Luna?* Oh, my Goddess, they called me their Luna!

"Alpha Christian told me to inform you that breakfast is ready in the dining room for you. He just got back from an early meeting."

So, that's where he was then.

"Could you take me there?" I asked.

The man smiled and nodded politely. "Of course. Follow me." As he showed me the way, I couldn't help but think about how he had called me a Luna. It was the female version of the Alpha: The Alpha's equal.

Christian's scent swarmed over me as we walked through two big, mahogany doors. I grinned as I spotted him sitting behind an elegant table with food set out perfectly. It was quiet, and he was the only one in here besides a servant pouring his coffee.

"Good morning," I called out.

He looked up from his newspaper, his eyes roaming my body as I walked in his direction. "Good morning..." he trailed off, slowly dropping the paper to the table.

"What?" I hesitantly asked, sitting next to him .

Christian folded his newspaper, never letting his stare waver as he asked, "You walked out there in front of unmated males like that?" I could see the gold flecks shining in his eyes as his wolf clawed at the surface.

I gulped, putting the cutlery that I had picked up back down with a clatter. "I didn't know the code to get back into the hall to change," I mumbled, suddenly feeling very exposed under his stare. I watched as he took off his suit jacket and handed it to me.

"I would just feel better if you wore that over your clothes when we head back up. You don't have to now." I nodded in understanding. He hadn't marked me yet, and until he did, any male attention towards me would only infuriate his wolf. Marking was something important in a mate bond, and without it, the male was usually very possessive. A mark was a bite to the neck, fully claiming the other as their own. It was generally done through a ceremony, or so my mother told me, but she was never appropriately marked herself, so couldn't be certain.

After relaxing in his seat again and picking his newspaper back up, it was silent. I made my plate, stacking a bunch of the pancakes on top of each other, but stopped halfway through pouring my syrup. "Chris?" I spoke, and he picked up his head to stare over his newspaper towards me, his eyes glowing with happiness.

"I like it when you call me that." I grinned, rolling my eyes. "But yes?"

"Mason's wolf eyes… they were red, but yours are gold. Are all alphas' eyes different?" I was curious because most of the regular wolves in the sectors pretty much had varying shades of "normal" yellows, I should say. I hadn't really ever seen other wolves with such vibrant eyes, so I wondered whether it had to do with their rank on the Personal Status System; if it was because they were Alphas and somehow better than your average wolf.

"Mason? You're on a first-name basis with him?" I pursed my lips, feeling a sigh bubbling in my throat.

"No. He's not around, so I don't have to use honorifics. Now, answer my question," I demanded playfully. He let out an amused growl, folding his newspaper back up for a second time. I picked up a strawberry and bit into its juicy flesh.

"Ok. To answer your question, yes, they're all different. My eyes show gold for my royal status. Mason's pack is War. War is bloody, hence his red eyes, or so I'm told. Alpha Jackson's are blue. It is often associated with depth and stability. It symbolizes wisdom, confidence, intelligence, and that's what the Intelligence Pack is. Alpha Ryker's are purple, believe it or not. Purple represents power," he informed.

I cocked an eyebrow, my pancakes forgotten, and the strawberries my new popcorn. "How is it like that? How'd it start?"

Chris folded his arms and painted a thoughtful look onto his features. "The story told is that a witch created a spell hundreds of years ago as revenge for a man that no longer loved her. She cursed him into worshipping the moon. Then, she cursed his best friends, to get at him more effectively, you could say." I nodded, picking up another strawberry and popping it into my mouth. Christian kept talking, but his eyes followed my every move. I listened to him, but I kept my eyes out for his piqued interest in my peripheral vision. How could I not?

Clearing his throat, Christian continued. "So, that's how the first Alphas were born. They figured out they could turn people, and soon a pack was created, but they fought against each other for power. They ended up breaking away from one another and making their own packs, stating themselves as Alphas. Each pack was small, but over the years, they grew as more werewolves delivered the gift, a bite that changes a human's life forever. As generations passed, with the help of a witch, a ritual was kept to pass down the Alpha title to an heir."

I tilted my head in fascination. "A ritual? With a witch? What kind? Is it hard? Super elaborate? Boring?"

Christian shrugged. "Nowadays, it's just a simple ceremony almost any witch can do. Though, if you're bringing up more powerful Alphas like Mason and the others, then you need a witch that is a descendant of the one who first created us. There are still two alive. One daughter went missing years back, but one is still up and about." Wow.

"Now that any witch can do the ceremony, are there any more Alphas out there?" I questioned him curiously.

He nodded. "Yes, but not only that. There are other packs, too." I gasped, now wholly forgetting about the strawberries.

"No way? I thought there were only four, including yours." He shook his head.

"There are smaller packs with Alphas who each have a status below the four original pack's Alphas. Honestly, I don't even know whether they're still alive. Members died off over the years, and they were just forgotten about. Most wolves who were of a higher status wanted to join the four most powerful packs, so many smaller packs have diminished or have become completely barren."

"That's crazy!" I exclaimed as he bit into a biscuit, nodding at my outburst. Leaning back into my chair, I felt my mind racing with new questions. I never knew this. It wasn't like we had any real knowledge about this kind of stuff in the sectors, so I was very much in awe at all of the new information. And I, of course, still had one more question I wanted to ask. "What were their names?"

"There are three that I remember. There was the Rampant Pack, which was a very careless pack. They cared more about the wolf's soul rather than the body that contained it. Then, there was the Immaculate Pack. They believed in cleanliness and purity. They established a set of divine rules that the pack had to follow to worship the Goddess properly. Lastly, there was a pack that many described as horrible and ruthless. They called themselves the Malevolent Pack. They were vicious, deceptive, and killed for fun. Many tried to put the pack out but failed. They were quite powerful." He willingly explained this information to me, and he seemed to be trying to keep me from getting overwhelmed, but I could feel myself starting to shake. Everything I thought I knew about this system was getting tossed and turned, molding into something completely different. It was all very new, very sudden, and fascinating. Almost terrifying.

"Then who stopped them if they were so powerful?" I asked.

"Me," he simply said, sitting back in his chair and resting his arms against the chair's armrests.

My jaw dropped. "W-what? What-what do you mean? How? What?!"

Christian let out a short chuckle at my perplexed expression and fish-like face, his eyes drifting off to the distance as he relived an old memory. "When I was seventeen, I was given the Alpha King title. A year later, the Malevolent Pack's killings were growing worse. Mason wasn't Alpha yet—his father was at the time. His father sent in hundreds of troops, but they were all slaughtered. That pack used some dark, dark magic, so I stepped in, fearing for our own kind," he reminisced, looking back towards me as if it pained him to be in that part of his head again. I brought my hand over and rested it on his arm, trying my best to comfort him. He had been so young.

"How did you beat them when they had dark magic on their side?" I asked softly, letting my thumb rub soothing circles over the long sleeve of his shirt.

"You can't kill a royal that easily," he informed, "especially when the first of our kind's blood is in your system. Let's just say I put an end to their Alpha, and they submitted to me. It took a year to get it under control, but it was worth it." He finally smiled, and I knew he could feel my pride for him.

Yet, I was still curious about something. "How old are you?"

"Twenty-six, and you?" he asked, putting his hand over my own. The contact of his warm hand over mine made me stop my rapid thoughts.

"I'm twenty-two," I replied, grinning childishly. *So, he's older.*

"Ah, I see," he grinned, pushing his chair back and standing to his feet. The action caused us to break contact, but he held out his hand for me to take.

"If you're done eating, I'd like to give you a proper tour." I nodded, smiling.

For a few hours, Christian showed me all around the palace and around the pack. It was beautiful, and I couldn't get enough of it. I was more than blessed to be in a place of such beauty. Though sadly, our day together came to an abrupt end when he was called into a meeting. Christian said I could continue to walk around, however.

I explored the gardens out back and maybe the kitchen again for my soggy pancakes and headed back towards the palace. I took a turn into the main foyer once I finished eating my late breakfast and went to head back upstairs when a girl appeared in front of me.

"Who do you think you are?" she sneered, growling in my face with shimmering eyes.

I looked around in confusion. "Uh, what?" She rolled her eyes, flipping her blonde hair over her shoulder. My eyebrows twitched up for half a second, my confusion and frustration both growing.

"I'm Amanda, the soon to be queen. Why are you hanging around my mate?" she snapped.

Christian

I didn't want to leave Scarlett, but I had an important meeting to attend to. Alpha Mason was on the other end of the conference call, while me, Axel, and my father sat around a table.

"The hunters are way out of control, we have to declare war and put a stop to them." Mason stated.

"What has happened now?" Dad asked.

"They have taken one of my members, Aurora Leigh, as a prisoner and are doing Goddess knows what to her. This is where I draw the line, Christian. They are coming after our own pack members like it's some kind of sick game. I know we've been apprehensive about starting a war, but it's our only option now. If we don't fight back, they will come for us all."

I sighed, folding my arms as I sat back in my chair. "I think you're right. It's time to get our men prepared, but I want to wait until after I introduce Scarlett as the soon-to-be queen before I announce a war. She's already nervous as it is, so I don't want to throw something else in the mix."

"Understood," Mason replied. "I will get the word out to my men and you should do the same. It's time we fight back and end all this horrible torture they are causing. We need to save our people."

"Agreed," Dad nodded.

"How is Alpha Jackson doing with our plans so far?" I asked.

"He's perfecting them as we speak. I talked to him yesterday and he believes he has something that will be very helpful when all this starts," Mason replied.

"Good, tell him to send everything over to me so I can take a look at it."

"Of course, is there anything else?"

"No, thank you for your time, Mason." he nodded, ending the call and I turned to my father with a tired look.

"You're doing the right thing. I know you hate the thought of a war, but it's in everyone's best interest. If we don't do something soon, we're going to be seen as weak, and you and I both know we are far from that."

I ran a hand over my face. "I know, and I understand. I just hate the thought of it. I just met my mate and knowing that a war is about to break out, I can't help but be worried for her safety."

"As you should be, Christian, but she is perfectly safe here and I know that no one, including myself, is going to let her be in harm's way."

I gave him a small smile. "I appreciate that."

"I know we don't always get along, but I also know how it feels to have a mate. You may not believe me, but I'm happy for you. Goddess knows you're going to be a better mate than I ever was," he spoke, bitterness lacing his tone at the last part.

I looked down, not wanting to think about the mistakes he made with my mother, and slowly stood up from my chair. "Speaking of Scarlett, I need to go find her. I let her roam the palace and lord knows what she's gotten herself into." I mused.

"I'll come with you. I need to head downstairs anyway."

We made our way down, heading to the living area, when I heard yelling.

My head snapped in that direction, seeing no other than Scarlett and Amanda in the midst of what looked like quite a heated argument. By the looks of it, Amanda wasn't taking our news well from our meeting early this morning.

My blood started to boil, and I took a step forward, but my father's arm shot out, stopping me. "This is a good time to see how she reacts, Christian. Let her do her thing. Let's see if she's already Luna material."

I reluctantly stayed back, watching from afar.

Scarlett

I crossed my arms and tried asking the girl with a straight voice and serious face, but instead, a snicker broke through my one-word question. "Mate?"

"Yes," she gritted out, her eyes darkening.

I licked my lips and uncrossed my arms, very patiently explaining. "I would just like to say that I don't even know who you are. I don't know if you've heard, but Christian found his *true* mate. Lastly, there's no need to get all mad just because you're no longer receiving a crown." My voice was mocking, and my head was high as I watched her gasp at having been spoken to like that. My wolf perked at her irritated look, feeling proud to finally tell some slimy little she-wolf that he was ours, that Christian was mine.

"He is mine! I am supposed to take the crown, not you!"

I snorted. "Amanda, it's over. You were just a placeholder until he found his legitimate mate. Jealousy is an ugly color darling, and it does not suit you."

She growled, and before I knew it, had pushed me by the shoulders with the force of her wolf, no doubt, knocking me backward and onto the ground. My wolf crawled to the surface, practically itching to be let out as I stared up at her in fury. Self-restraint, Scarlett. Not yet.

"Si quieres pelear lo podemos hacer afuera." I spoke in a sharp tone. She laughed at me, like I was merely joking around.

"You act as if I understand what you're saying or if I care. *You're stupido.* Do you understand that?" she mocked, making my blood *boil.*

"I said, if you want to fight, we can go outside." I snapped.

Her eyes widened as I was up in a flash and stalking towards her. I felt my canines extend, and my claws break through my fingernails. I channeled my wolf and allowed her a sip of fresh air, but only so much.

"Don't ever speak about my mate, nor lay your hands on me again. I may be a girl from the sectors, and I may be a Latina, but if being either has taught me one thing, it's how to fight." I snarled, roughly grabbing her by the shirt.

"Scarlett!" I heard and felt an arm pull me away and into a chest. I grasped control instantly and relaxed as my wolf retreated into the depths of my mind.

When I could see clearly, I stared up at Chris apologetically, kind of embarrassed at my temper, and slightly tense at how he might react at my outburst. "I'm sorry, I just-" But he cut me off.

"Calm down and take in some deep breaths, Scarlett." Christian's voice soothed my nerves and remaining anger as I rested my head against his shoulder in relief. He rubbed another round of soothing shapes on my back but whipped towards the girl almost violently. "If you ever lay your hands on my mate again, you will not live to see another day. Father and I have already told you. It's off. There is nothing between us, and there will never be," he snapped as her eyes widened, welling up with tears.

"But Christian!" she whined, and I growled at her persistence. The girl just couldn't take a hint, could she?

"Go," he said, and she obediently followed her Alpha's command, retreating up the stairs.

Once she was gone, I stepped out of his grasp, even though I really didn't want to, and sheepishly asked, "You saw that?"

He sighed and pulled my embarrassed self back into him, kissing my forehead. "I did. It took everything in me not to come over and banish her from the pack when she laid her hands on you," he confessed, and I closed my eyes, feeling both pleased and impossibly more embarrassed. If my mother were here, she would have hit me with her chancla at my childish behavior.

Christian seemed to find my embarrassment at his arrival slightly amusing as he added, "I was with my father coming down the hall when it happened. He wanted to see what you would do." My eyes widened when I looked up at him.

"Don't worry. You passed the test. He was pleased. He even said you'd make a great Luna with the way you stood up for us both," he grinned as a small smile crawled onto my face. *His dad likes me!*

"When will I meet him?" I asked, and he shrugged. I couldn't help but notice that his expression changed as if the thought of us meeting was an unpleasant one.

"You don't want me to?" I questioned, and he shook his head.

"No, it's not that. My father and I don't have a good relationship. He has lied to me. Let's just say that, and I'll never forgive him for it, but let's forget all that for right now, okay?" I just nodded, not wanting to press the matter anymore, no matter how curious I was.

"I still can't believe you saw that." I grumbled, and he chuckled.

"It was quite entertaining how feisty you got. Though I had to interfere when you channeled your wolf, which was amazing, by the way." he smirked as my cheeks heated up. "Don't even get me started on you speaking Spanish. Goddess, that was hot. I thought you said you didn't know the language?" My cheeks reddened even more.

"No, I said I know some."

"Speak it," he grinned.

"No," I laughed out, slightly pushing him away.

"Please? I'll speak Italian." How can he be even hotter?

"You know Italian?" I asked.

"My family is Italian. Throughout our history, we just moved here," he explained, and I grinned.

"Only if you go first."

He squinted his eyes at me and nodded. He has a devilish grin as he stated the foreign words to me, and I think I almost died right there on the spot.

"What does that mean?" I greedily asked him as he leaned in closer.

"I really want to kiss you...."

"Dios, ayúdame." *Lord help me.*

CHAPTER EIGHT

———◆◇◆———

Scarlett

He's going to kiss me; he's going to kiss me.... Alpha Christian was going to kiss me! Scarlett Madison, kissing the royal Alpha—the king! I was not prepared for this today, but who was complaining? *Definitely not me.*

He was looking into my eyes with an intense emotion I couldn't quite grasp. My breath hitched as he leaned closer, causing my heart to leap with joy. His lips were centimeters from mine, so close that I could feel his warm breaths and smell his crisp aftershave. I wanted him just to let go and smash his lips onto mine, but he hesitated, stopping just a hair's breadth away.

I was about to throw all the self-control my mother tried teaching me to the wind and close the gap between us for him when I heard a high pitch squeal. I jumped, taking a shaky step away from Christian to see a girl with an excited grin making her way towards us. Christian let out a growl of annoyance and turned to glare at her. So, that explained the hesitation. He'd heard her coming.

"Cora? What are you doing here?" He asked.

"I knew it! I just knew it! Father told me you'd found your mate! I knew it would happen! Oh, Christian, I'm so happy for you!" Her voice was booming and seemingly riddled with a thick accent. As she got closer, her smile was growing, and when she was close enough, she threw her toned arms around him.

"How rude of me!" she gasped, pulling away from him to give me her already signature big grin. "I'm Cora, this brat's sister," she introduced herself, sticking her hand out. I smiled, shaking it happily.

"Scarlett," I replied, carefully watching her as she looked between me and Christian.

She gave him a knowing look and a little nod of her head before she told him, "She's gorgeous." I blushed, looking down. Christian nodded back, pulling me to his chest.

With the howl of a thousand she-wolves, Cora erupted into another bat of squeals before exclaiming, "We have to go shopping! I want to get to know my future sister-in-law!" That actually sounded fun, but I had no money.

"That's a great idea. I have to meet with some people tonight to establish a certain meeting." Christian said, and my eyebrows raised curiously. "I'm getting all the packs together… Think of it as a huge ball. It's to announce you as my mate and the future Queen." Great, another thing to be nervous about.

He's showing you off as his mate! What is there to be nervous about, Scarlett? Get a hold of yourself!

A second later, Christian dug into his back pocket, pulling out his wallet and handing me a sleek black card. "Take it and buy whatever you desire. I mean it." I shook my head, pushing the card back to him.

"I can't," I replied, and he just gave me a small grin.

"I'm not taking no for an answer, and just to show you that..." he handed the card to Cora, and her eyes lit up as the card touched her eager hands.

"Girl's day out! Come on!" she cried, grabbing my arm.

"She's changing first!" Christian vehemently demanded first. Cora laughed, pulling me towards the stairs.

"Of course, your majesty." she mocked, dragging me up the stairs with the speed of a cheetah.

I didn't know whether to love her enthusiasm or be terrified of it.

***

I groaned for the hundredth time. Six hours of shopping. SIX. "Is all this necessary?" I asked Cora, looking at all the bags littering the ground around us. *She's definitely crazy.*

"Obviously." We were walking around the huge mall, and the many stores— the costly brand stores— when I was about to collapse from the weight of our twentieth store's box of heeled boots, Cora had insisted I buy for myself.

"I'm hungry and tired," I complained, tiredly scooping up the bags I had dropped. She was carrying just as many items as me, but she was barely breaking a sweat. Probably the royal blood in her. *That's right, Scarlett, her superior genes that you definitely don't have.*

"Christian sent me two things to get you, and that's all we have left," she informed me.

"What are they?" I asked, steadying myself after almost tripping over one of the dangling bags slipping down my left arm.

"A phone and a ball gown."

I paused, staring at the back of her head with the most exasperated look I could muster. "But we've already spent so much." Every time she swiped the card greedily, I would cringe just the slightest, and a little bit of my sanity would crack—every single time. If my mom and dad were shopping, they would have taken me to some thrift store with a magazine full of coupons to purchase last season's clothes. This was way too much—getting all these fancy and expensive clothes were not my social norm.

"Please, you probably didn't even make a dent into his account. To him, we barely took a penny out." Goddess, how much money did he have?

A second later, Cora was turning towards a brightly lit shop that held beautiful gowns. I felt my heart sink as I took in all the gowns on display in the front window. They were all stunning and covered in eye-catching sequins. Without even realizing it, my face screwed up into a cringe, and I felt myself running to catch up with Cora. With adrenaline now running through my blood, I threw my arm out and caught one of the bags on Cora's shoulder, effectively stopping her pursuit. Bringing her close to me, I whispered to her, "They're extremely expensive."

"That's the point!" she whispered back with a laugh as she pushed me into the store. She followed me, immediately heading for various gowns hanging from a rack to her right. I awkwardly watched her, trying not to mess anything up. Goddess knows if I accidentally destroyed a dress, we would have had to pay for it! I didn't have that kind of will-power, unlike Cora. I watched as her arms became entangled by a monsoon of dresses—red, blue, emerald, pink—all gorgeous. By that time, our bags of clothes had all been pushed to one corner of the store.

With a hefty amount of dresses on her, Cora turned towards me and all but threw me into a changing room, demanding I try on all the dresses she had picked out. I tried on a blue one, which she said didn't show my curves enough, so I tried on a green one, which apparently didn't make my eyes pop. By the fifth 'no' on a dress, I wanted to give up, go home, and eat. I could just wear the dress my mom had bought me for my twenty-first birthday last year. I thought it would have been fine, at least, but Cora kept insisting, practically running all over the store, trying to find the perfect one.

"Cora," I groaned as she stuffed one more dress into my arms, this one particularly heavy.

"Just try it on. I think it will be good. Plus, it's gold, so it'll go well with us royals." I shook my head, closing the door of the dressing room with a groan.

Once I had managed to get it on, I looked into the mirror to see how bad this dress would be compared to the last thousand dresses I had tried on; but as soon as I saw my reflection, my eyes widened in shock. I actually liked it. It hugged my waist and flowed at the bottom, giving me just enough skin to show off, but not too much, of course.

I opened the door, and Cora's eyes widened. "Yes! That's the one! We're getting it." she cheered, clapping her hands together.

"Thank Goddess, food!" I cried out, and she laughed.

"Come on. I'll buy you some dinner."

"Now that's the best news I've heard all day."

When Cora and I got home after eating an equally expensive dinner, at least four palace workers had to help us carry bags in. Christian was going to kill us.

"I had so much fun! I really feel like you are going to make a wonderful Luna to this pack and a Queen to all wolves." My heart melted at her kind words.

"That means a lot."

"Of course! If you ever need anything, let me know. We need to hang out again. Unfortunately, I have to travel to the Intelligence Pack to help assist with their police management. The criminal activity has risen more violently, and my brother has asked me to take care of the situation." She gave me a sad look, but I held my hand up.

"I understand! When you get back, we totally will!"

"Fantastic! See you soon." She air-kissed my cheeks and headed out as a lonely guard trailed behind her with a tower of shoe boxes wobbling in his arms.

After watching her leave, I sighed and looked around at all my new possessions. This is going to be a pain to put away. Either way, I got right to work. About an hour into my unpacking, I felt two arms circle around my waist from behind.

"I see shopping went well." Christian murmured, and I grinned.

"Your sister is a shopaholic."

"Indeed, she is." I turned around to face him and wrapped my arms around his neck.

"How was the meeting?"

"It was okay. The ball is in three days. Invitations are being sent out currently so the Alphas can arrange a convoy to the palace." he said, staring down at me.

"That's going to be a lot of people," I stated, causing him to chuckle.

"The Alpha selects people to come. There will be a couple of hundred there, but we don't mind. There's plenty of room."

I nodded and sighed. "I have so many bags. Why would you give Cora your card? I tried saying no, but she just kept swiping."

He let out a hearty laugh, bringing me closer into his chest. "You're too cute. I gave it to her because I knew you wouldn't accept it. How many times do I have to tell you, what's mine is yours, darling?" His new nicknames were growing on me. I had to admit.

"I know, I know, but I don't want anyone thinking I'm taking advantage of you."

Chris held me by my shoulders, his eyes crinkled with understanding as he said, "Who cares what people think, Scar? I know I don't. Please, don't let people get to you. They say stuff to try and bring you down because they're jealous, and you can't let them."

"Wise words."

He grinned at me, shrugging like it was no big deal. "I know." We both let out a small laugh, but then his face became more serious. "You're happy here, aren't you?" he asked with a hint of uncertainty.

I tilted my head up at him and gave him a pleased smile to convey how I felt. "Very much, Chris. I'm with my mate; there's nothing better. Plus, my family will be happy and taken care of again." He smiled back at me in relief, and not even a moment later, I saw how his gaze dropped down to my lips.

"Oh, will you just kiss me, you idiot?"

His lips met mine in a swift motion. It was like nothing I'd ever felt before. Those wretchedly enticing tingles shot through the skin of my lips. My toes curled, and an audible whimper of pure pleasure escaped from the back of my throat. A possessive growl rumbled in his chest as he pulled me closer, deepening the kiss so much, my back was arching, and he had to use his arms to steady me. I could feel his fingers digging into my sides, but I couldn't care less as I threaded my fingers through his hair, tugging just the slightest bit. That seemed to set him off because I felt my back hit the wall behind me, not even a second later, but as soon as it started, it ended. We both had to break apart for air. He rested his forehead against mine, our chests just barely brushing up against each other as we gulped in the much-needed oxygen.

"Wow," he mumbled.

"Wow," I repeated, and he grinned down at me with his beautiful eyes and just-kissed lips. Was it hot in here, or was it just me?

"I'm going to go take a quick shower while you finish up. Is that okay?" he asked, and I nodded, pursing my lips to keep the suddenly dirty thoughts of him taking a shower out of my head.

"Of course." I watched his figure retreat to the bathroom, and the door closed behind him.

"A cold shower." I snickered as I bit my lip.

"Heard that!" he called out, and I threw my head back as I laughed out loud on my way back to putting things away. Just as I had sat down to fold the new shirts, I broke out into a sudden sweat. To be precise, I felt like I was burning up as if I had a fever or the room was on fire.

Setting down a shirt mid-fold, I used my hands to fan cool air onto my face. When that stopped working, or should I say when I realized it wasn't helping at all, I got to my feet and went into the kitchen, grabbing a cup from the cabinet and filling it up with some cold water. I gulped the water down, but it felt like as soon as the water was in my mouth, it was boiling. Maybe I should change out of this fuzzy sweater?

I quickly changed into a tank top I'd bought and felt much better. Minutes later, the shower cut off, and Christian walked out in only a pair of sweatpants, and I couldn't help but look at his well-defined chest. I managed to look away and go into the closet to put some shirts up before he knew I was staring and unintentionally feeding into his ego. As I finished putting away the shirts, though, the warmth I was feeling earlier crawled back up onto my skin.

"Hey, Chris?" I called out.

"Yeah?" he called from the kitchen.

"Could you adjust the AC? I'm a little toasty."

"Sure thing, babe."

CHAPTER NINE

―◆◇◆―

Scarlett

I woke up sweating and felt utterly disgusted. Why was it so hot in here? Throwing the covers off, I walked into the kitchen, and my eyes moved towards Christian's bedroom door. I sighed, opening the fridge and grabbed some milk. After I poured myself a glass, I had to tie my hair up to keep the wet strands from sticking to the back of my neck. I walked over to the balcony of the penthouse and opened the doors. A cold breeze hit my sweaty skin, and satisfaction washed over me. I needed a walk.

After walking back into the penthouse, I tugged on a coat and grabbed my milk, heading out the door. I made my way downstairs and walked outside to the garden, sighing in relief when the cold air hit me again. It felt wonderful. I took a seat on a bench and gazed up at the stars. I was sure it was probably two in the morning, but I could have cared less. It was beautiful out.

"Luna?" I heard and turned to see Christian's Beta, the second in command here in the pack, walking up to me.

"Yes?" I asked.

"What are you doing out here? I was walking back from the packhouse and saw you. It would be best if you come inside. It's not safe to be out this late."

I gave him a small nod and stood up. "I was getting some fresh air. Thank you, Beta," I said awkwardly, not knowing his name.

"I understand. Please, call me Axel," he replied respectfully and bowed his head, moving to the side so I could pass him. As I walked by him, a sharp pain struck me in my side, causing me to gasp.

"Everything okay?" Axel asked, moving before me with a concerned look.

"Yeah. I think I just-*ah*!" I cried out, falling to my knees as another ache came.

"Guards!" he called out and went down to help me but froze.

I looked up, seeing his eyes cloud over. No. Oh, Goddess, no. *I'm in heat.* I looked up to the sky, seeing the full moon shining brightly above. How could I have been so stupid?

He stared at me with intense hunger and started backing up. As the guards approached, he held up his hand to stop them. "Don't touch her," he growled out as if he were battling with himself to stay away. Any unmated male was attracted to a female in heat, meaning they couldn't resist.

"Christian!" I screamed at the top of my lungs, praying he would hear me. I was in too much pain to move.

The guards' eyes were filled with lust, and I tried to stand but screamed out in pain. As one guard stepped forward, Axel growled and shoved him back.

"Leave!" he yelled at them, but it wasn't helping. They weren't listening because their wolf had already taken over. They weren't as strong as Axel to fight their wolf down. I looked at Axel pleadingly, the pain inside of me intensifying, but my fear growing deeper.

"Please," I sobbed out. I didn't even know what I was pleading for at this point. Stop the pain? Get me to Christian? Something. I could see the internal battle with himself, but he took a deep breath and walked over, wrapping an arm around me.

"Come on. I'm getting you out of here." He bared his teeth at the guards, and they submitted quickly, all of them backing away with their heads bowed and tails between their legs.

I started to stand and felt the pain ease from the male attention my body was craving. We began to walk back into the palace, but as I looked over at him, I could see his jaw clenching. I looked away, sorry for both of us, but my vision started to become blurry again, and seconds later, I had to sit on the back steps that led into the palace. The Beta, Axel, was distancing himself from me, putting his hands on his head as he started to pace back and forth a couple of steps below me.

"I can't help you. I'm sorry. I-I can't get you to Christian like I thought I could. My control is dwindling by the second. I mind-linked him, though."

The door swung open, and I saw another man stand there. Of course, he was unmated, too.

"Look, man, I know your control is slipping, but she's the Alpha's mate. If you go anywhere near her, he will kill you." Axel warned, but the man's attention was already on me.

"I don't care." The man started to approach me, and my eyes widened in fear.

"Take one more step, and I won't hesitate to end you." a deep voice spoke, causing the man to freeze.

My heart leaped as Christian came into sight. He quickly made his way towards me and scooped me up. "I'm here, Scarlett." he cooed, whispering more soothing words into my ear as he carried me into the palace and back upstairs.

"It hurts," I whimpered painfully as another wave hit me. It felt like I was dying. Sweat drenched my back and forehead, needle-like stabbing pains raked over my sides, and I could do nothing but cry out in agony.

"I know," he murmured, wrapping his arms around me tighter. The contact from my mate was helping, but only so much. My wolf was happy, though, as her real mate finally had arrived to help.

Once we made it back into the penthouse, he rushed towards the bathroom and sat me on the counter. He turned towards the shower and blasted the cold water. "Come on," he mumbled, shuffling my arms out of my coat, and picking me up off the counter. With me still being held in his arms, he walked me into the shower.

Both of our clothes were drenched, but I couldn't seem to find the time to think about that. The heat was calming down as he held me, and we sunk to the ground, the water pouring over us did wonders, but I was still aching.

"Thank you," I whispered, relieved that the pain was starting to go away, that the heat was slowly easing. He just clenched his jaw and nodded. I could tell he was fighting his wolf back. It was hard for an unmated male to go against the mating ritual, especially if they were in their mate's presence.

I rested my palm against his shirt and stared up at him, sadness starting to make its way into my heart as I took in the state he was putting himself into for me. "I'm sorry," I mumbled.

"Don't be. You can't help this," he gritted out, placing a kiss on my forehead; and like that, we sat under the cold stream of water falling from the showerhead. I had put my ear against his quickly beating heart, and he had rested his dripping cheek atop my wet hair. It would have been a funny sight to me if I had been in the right state of mind.

"Are you feeling better?" he asked after a time of silence.

"Yes. Much."

"Good. Do you think you can get changed and into bed?" he asked softly, adjusting his legs, which were on either side of me as I rested between them. If I had been in my normal state, I would have been blushing like a dummy, feeling super awkward, but I could only feel thankful. The contact was helping me wherever I could get it.

"I can try," I admitted, pulling myself up to my feet. Christian nodded and helped me stand, as well. He led me out of the bathroom after turning off the shower but let me walk to my room and into my closet myself. There, I changed out of my soaked clothes only to feel the familiar heat crawl up my spine. After I changed, I walked to his bedroom. I felt shy as I gazed down at his lying form on the bed. He was obviously tired, and it was all because of me.

Christian must have felt my discomfort because he opened his eyes and turned to stare at my trembling body. He scooted over and patted the spot next to him, saying invitingly, "Come here, sweetheart." I smiled and walked over to him, crawling up next to him. He instantly wrapped his arms around me, and I did the same.

"How long is this going to last?" I asked.

"Until the full moon is over. It shouldn't be as bad tomorrow."

I nodded, tightening my grip around him. "I'm sorry I can't give you what you want," I said, and he looked down at me.

"And what exactly is that?" His eyebrows furrowed in confusion.

"You know..." I drifted off, and he let out a laugh.

"I'm not with you because I want sex, Scarlett. You're my mate. You're the person I'm destined to be with, love, support, and start a family with. Whatever you feel like doing, I'm okay with."

I smiled, thanking him, but another wave decided to come on and ruin the moment. The pain attacked my lower sides, making me cringe and shift uncomfortably. "Ow," I sniffled, crinkling my fingers into Christian's shirt.

"I'm sorry, hopefully, this will all be over soon." he apologized, bringing me even closer to him.

CHAPTER TEN

◆◇◆

Scarlett

Tonight was the night of the ball, and to say I was nervous would be an understatement. There were so many people coming, most of which I had never met. I only knew Christian, of course, and Alpha Mason and Elizabeth if she was even allowed to come. Christian was used to the whole meeting new people and being in crowded situations, but I wasn't. I was terrified. I hated family reunions, for crying out loud!

While I was pacing around, afraid out of my mind, Chris was sound asleep in his bedroom. He was no doubt exhausted from the previous nights since I had started my heat. *I could curse the full moon.* Nothing had happened, really, just the fact that I was always in pain and unable to leave my room. He was there, too, every second of this excruciating experience. Whenever he had to go for even a brief meeting, the pain was at its worst, so he had a female worker watch over me during parts of the day when he was off doing Alpha duties.

Last night hadn't been too bad, but neither of us had been able to sleep until the early hours, and when I woke up this morning, he was knocked out. He didn't even hear a different female worker knocking on the door. I did, so I let her in to do my hair after I showered in the guest bathroom. It was probably the first time someone had done my hair since my mom made me go on a date with Peter Scott when I was sixteen.

So, this was the real deal. I wanted to do something simple to introduce myself, but no, Christian was going all out. 'Anything for my Queen' he would say whenever I brought it up.

I heard the bathroom door open and in walked Christian, who looked half asleep. I covered my grin as I stared at his bed head.

"You didn't wake me," he mumbled.

"I wanted you to get some sleep."

He smiled, walking over to snake his hands around my waist. "Shouldn't I be saying that to you?" he asked, and I shrugged, resting my small hands over his larger hands as he softly swayed us.

"Maybe."

"You look beautiful," he whispered in my ear, studying me. I wasn't even in my dress yet, but I smiled as he leaned down to give me a soft yet passionate kiss. He pulled away, and I saw the gold specks wanting to come out in his eyes as his wolf clawed to the surface.

"Well, we got through your first heat together. That's a big step." he joked, managing to evoke a laugh from me.

"The biggest."

He let out a laugh of his own, kissing the top of my head. "I'm going to go ahead and shower. Feel free to join me." he winked.

"Oh, I'll get right on that," I mused as I walked towards my bedroom door, hearing his soft chuckle behind me. I closed the door behind me and walked to my closet, seeing my gorgeous gold dress laid out with gold heels to match.

I prayed I didn't face-plant.

***

After the long process of Christian and me getting ready, we made our way down to the ballroom where everyone was gathered. We walked in from a back door, hoping no one would notice us just yet. My stomach turned at the sight before me.

It was packed. Christian wanted to talk with people first before introducing me to see how people interacted with me; therefore, we split up. I was currently sitting by the punch bowl, nervously sipping on a cup of the red liquid. I had yet to talk to anyone. I felt like I was back at the sector's dance they used to throw for the kids to get their minds off things. I'd always stand awkwardly by the food table, pretty much doing this same thing. Why are you so awkward, Scarlett?

A girl in a gorgeous, puffy, red dress walked up, pouring herself a glass. Her blonde hair was pinned to perfection, and I was jealous.

"She must be some lucky girl," she said to me, and I couldn't help but grin.

"She is..." I dragged out, feeling a funny little bubble form in my stomach.

"Do you think she's stuck up or in it for the money?" she asked while sipping her drink.

"No! I- I mean, I would hope not." I quickly covered, bringing my drink up to cover my panicked eyes.

She let out a little laugh as she spoke. "I know. I want our Queen to be devoted to us wolves, and him, of course. A happy King and Queen make us a happy kingdom." I stared at her in awe.

"She will be. I promise."

She turned, looking at me skeptically. Then she shrugged. "One can only hope. I'm Octavia," she introduced herself, sticking her hand out. I grabbed it and shook it with as much Queen-like grace that I could muster.

"Call me Scarlett."

"Rings a bell," she mumbled to herself, and I wanted to laugh. "Have we met?"

"No, I don't believe so. What pack are you from?" I asked.

"Oh, Power Pack. Alpha Ryker."

I nodded, having seen the Alpha talking amongst others across the room. I was kind of curious if his eyes were really purple when he turned, but I kept my intrusive thoughts to myself.

"He saved my life not too long ago. There was a shooting," she explained and pulled up her dress a little, showing off a bullet wound, "Luckily, he showed up on time. He's an excellent Alpha."

"Oh, my Goddess." I gasped, and she nodded, dropping the end of the dress.

"The hunters are getting bad. I heard the King met with Alpha Mason, which can only mean war." The thought shook me to my core.

I was about to say something when I saw Christian making his way towards us.

"Ready, Scarlett?" he asked as he reached us. I smiled up at him and nodded.

"Yes," I mumbled softly, glancing at Octavia, who looked like a deer caught in headlights.

"I promise I will not let you down." I pledged to her as he pulled me away, watching her as she stood shocked.

"Friend?" Christian asked, and I shrugged.

"Maybe," I admitted, hoping that it would become true one day. He smiled, pulling me up the stairs with him. When we got to the top of the ballroom balcony, the sound of music and people's chatter quieted down.

"Everyone, you were called here for an important reason. To see the introduction and celebration of my mate, Scarlett Madison!" Everyone let out cheers as he wrapped his arm around me. "She's made me happier these past few days than I've ever been in my life. I know she'll make you all happy and proud." The crowd awed, and I blushed, looking at my shoes in complete embarrassment. "Let's celebrate! Please, feel free to come and greet your soon to be Queen!" he smiled widely, taking my hand to lead us down to the crowd.

Everyone was so lovely, and the greetings were memorable. I was honored to take on the position of Queen for these people. Although, I couldn't help but notice a group of girls with envious glares glancing towards me, their eyes like daggers. I tried not to look so bothered, but when I noticed that they were the friends of Amanda, my jaw instantly clenched, and my fists curled, ready to defend myself if need be. My wolf was already pacing within me, her guard up at the possible enemies.

"Ignore them," Christian whispered in my ear, one of his hands wrapping around one of my fists. I nodded, allowing my wolf to relax and my shoulders to fall as I gave him a small, reassuring smile.

Besides that, we danced, laughed, and just had an amazing time. I know tonight had been amazing, but in the back of my mind, I couldn't get Christian going to war off my mind. So, after the ball, I asked him about it as we laid on his bed.

"You met with Mason about war?" I asked, and he tensed.

"You catch on quickly, but yes. The hunters are overstepping," he confessed, tightening his arms around me.

"When?" I asked, barely above a whisper.

"Tomorrow, troops are being sent out."

"Are you going with them?"

"I'm hoping it won't come to that. Alpha Jackson is the smartest man I know, and he has a plan. Hopefully, that will give us a win, but if not, I'm going in. I'll have to."

"Please be careful. I- I can't lose you now that I have you." I expressed through misty eyes, and he placed a gentle kiss on my forehead.

"You'll never lose me." he stated matter-of-factly, but I didn't reply because I knew he couldn't promise that. Nobody could.

"My parents are coming to the Power Pack tomorrow." I changed the subject.

Christian nodded, "I know. Let's hope your dad likes me," he joked.

"He will," I skeptically said, not even believing my own words. There was a slight possibility, however. I mean, my mom loved him, and I thought she was going to murder him when she found out. I was wrong there, so maybe I was wrong about my father's feelings towards my mate, but as I bit my bottom lip in thought, bringing my hand up to scratch at my head, I highly doubted that. As I lost myself in my thoughts, I could feel Christian gazing down at me. I paused mid-thought, my eyes swiveling up to stare back at him, only to be caught off guard with the way he was looking at me, with such an intense emotion that I couldn't quite grasp.

"You're so beautiful," he murmured, slowly trailing his hand up my arm, over my shoulder, and finally resting it on my heated cheek as he continued, "stay with me tonight."

"Okay."

"Really?" His eyes lit up as bright as a thousand stars, "I thought I was going to have to beg." I let out a laugh at his happy state.

"I think I sleep better when you're around," I confessed, causing him to smile warmly down at me.

"Me too."

CHAPTER ELEVEN

---◆◇◆---

Scarlett

I woke up to an arm wrapped tightly around my waist. Smiling, I turned, facing Christian. He looked just as handsome sleeping as he did awake. Without realizing, I brought my hand up and slowly traced his cheekbone, continuing down his neck. Seconds later, his eyes fluttered open, a sleepy grin appearing on his face.

"I could wake up to that every day," he mumbled in a husky morning voice.

"Really now?" I asked, unable to wipe my grin off my face.

"Really," he agreed, pulling me closer and burying his face into my neck to attack me with kisses. I let out a squeal as I wriggled in his arms.

"Stop!" I laughed out.

"Never!" he declared, continuing his assault as I kept giggling.

"Christian!" I yelled out again, and he finally listened, pulling away to give me a goofy smile.

"Couldn't resist," he teased.

I chuckled, rolling my eyes as I kicked his comforter off my legs to get up, but was stopped by two very heavy hands. "I'm starving. Let me up."

"No, stay," he whined, enclosing me in his toned arms and pulling me close to his chest.

"What are you? Five?"

He shrugged, taking a second to think before replying, "Mostly." I deadpanned, giving him my best puppy-eyed stare. "Fine, but I'm cooking for you," he said, and I raised my eyebrows in surprise. "Yes, I know how to cook," he grumbled playfully, reading my mind.

I smiled innocently at him. "I was never thinking that," I fake gasped, and he let out a laugh as he got up.

"Whatever."

We made our way into the kitchen, and I sat on a barstool, watching him as he got right to work. He pulled down pots and pans, conjured up some ingredients he had gotten some of the kitchen staff to supply us with while I was under the weather, and started to cook. He moved around effortlessly, and I have to admit, he looked good doing it.

I didn't think I'd ever been this happy. If I had told myself a week before that I would be mated to Alpha Christian, the one Alpha I probably had the harshest dislike towards because of his elders, I wouldn't have believed a word.

Shaking my head, I stood from the stool and walked over to the living room, grabbing the TV remote, and switching the TV on. Like a thunderclap during a rainstorm, a blaring alert system blasted through the quiet penthouse. I dropped the remote immediately like it was a hot potato and covered my sensitive ears, swearing up and down from the shock. In seconds, Christian was by my side, looking at the TV.

"This is your news broadcast system. As of May, twenty-fifth, a war has been declared by King Christian and Alpha Mason against the hunters of America. Troops are stationed in these areas. Please listen closely to the following..." I drowned the rest out as I blankly stared at the TV.

This was really happening. My mind started spinning as I nervously chewed at my lower lip. This couldn't happen! I turned away from the monotonous news anchor to calm myself, but I couldn't help but worry about the one area I knew wasn't mentioned: the sectors. They had no pack for protection. They had nothing but their families, and some didn't even have that.

"Christian," I started, trying to make myself seem tough and demanding when I really only felt shaky, "you have to send troops to guard the sectors."

He directed his attention towards me with a confused look. "Why?" he asked. I stared at him bewildered, my mouth dropping open in hysteria.

I threw my hands up in exasperation. "Why?! *Why*?! Because while these perfect little packs are protected and guarded, the sectors are defenseless. It's not fair!" I exploded, suddenly being flooded with memories from my childhood in the sectors. I remembered all the times my family barely got help from the emergency services during a crime spree in our area, or when a nasty storm hit our part of the neighborhood, and a lot of the houses were damaged. Not to mention the food shortage, but once again, no one did anything!

Nobody ever cares about the sectors, and deep down, I knew the reason for that. I knew we were looked upon as the rejects, as the castaways that didn't belong to a pack because we weren't good enough or fortunate enough.

"They already are deemed not good enough for a pack, but now they don't even get a little bit of comfort or safety from war? You're incurable." I finished, turning to walk towards the guest bedroom, but Christian leaped out and caught onto my arm.

"Don't be mad at me, Scarlett, we just can't send any more troops out," he tried to reason with me, terrible reasoning if you ask me, so I turned towards him, scoffing.

"You know," my voice felt choked, and I couldn't control the frustrated tears that wanted to fall down my cheeks, "I lived in the sectors. I grew up in one of the worst ones, actually. I was in Sector C. The gates are rotted, and rogues easily get in and slaughter people... people I knew died almost like clockwork every month because everybody just stands by and does nothing. Now think about how easy it would be for hunters." Christian just stared at me through my rant with an unreadable expression as I continued, "How would you feel if you hadn't moved my parents up and I was visiting them, and all of a sudden, hunters decided to attack. How would you feel if I got hurt? If my family got hurt? If I was killed?"

He growled, his eyes flickering to gold, and his claws elongating into my skin. "I wouldn't let that happen."

I tried to rip my arm out of his grasp, but his hold was too strong, so I kept going, ignoring the slight sting in my arm and the sobs that were threatening to spill through my words. "Oh! Better yet, what if we had never even met? Then I was killed trying to protect my s-sister from a silver bullet headed straight for her heart! Then you never would have had the chance to meet me." his growls grew louder, and his grip tighter, but I couldn't feel it anymore. I was too lost in the what-ifs I was creating in my mind. "But that doesn't matter because the wolves in the sectors are just nobodies without a title. Some king you are. You definitely care about your kind." I snapped back to reality, throwing my head up to glare at the stupid idiot tearing me apart from the inside out.

"Enough!" Christian let out a furious roar, but I stood my ground, not even flinching, not even to wipe away the flood of tears blurring my vision as he softened his tone, "I've never had to see things from a different point of view, Scarlett, I didn't know how bad things truly are there, okay? I didn't know…"

"Then what are you doing just sitting here?! Why have you sat around all this time even before the war!" I snarled, breaking myself from his hold and making my way to the guest room to compose myself in its confinements. This time, he didn't stop me.

Today was supposed to be a good day! I was supposed to see my parents and surprise my father. I needed to contact them. Doing so, I quickly pulled out my phone and called my mom. On the third ring, she answered our house phone.

"Hello?" she asked with a worried voice.

"Mom, you have to leave the sectors and go to the Power Pack *now*. You need to explain to dad everything that has been happening. I know we wanted to surprise him about the move, but there's no time." I rushed out.

"I know," her soft voice drifted through the static line, sounding almost sad and sorry. I was about to ask her what was wrong when she started speaking again, "I can't leave my friends in this, Scar. Your father won't either. We have to stand our ground and fight back." she uttered, and my heart dropped.

"No! No, absolutely not! Look, I'll beg Christian to bring troops there. Please just go to the Power Pack. I cannot lose you, dad, or Ashlee." I stated through clenched teeth.

"A hunter was in our section today. He was close to injuring someone, but the men stopped him. We've been doing this for years. We can take care of ourselves. I'm sorry, Scarlett, I love you. I'll see you soon."

"No, wait! You don't understand the new threat these hunters are-" The line went dead, and I let the phone drop from my hands in a panic.

No, no! This couldn't be happening! I darted to the bedroom door, throwing it open. I had to do something.

"Christian!" I cried out, but he was nowhere to be seen. I grabbed my head, unable to grasp everything that was happening, but paused after hearing the news broadcast siren.

"This is your news broadcast system update. Riots are breaking out from the humans. The first set of troops have been in contact with hunters. Nineteen wolves are counted dead. Injured is unknown. Hunters' deaths are estimated to be at thirty-seven, the number of injured still unknown. King Christian is sending new troops out as of six minutes ago in the following locations: the Sectors A, B, and C. Sector D is being relocated. Royal guards are being posted around the perimeters."

My heart skipped a beat; he listened. The faint 'your wish is my command' ran through my head. *He meant it.*

Turning the TV off, I sat down, taking a deep breath to try and calm myself. How bad was this going to get?

The sound of the door unlocking grabbed my attention. I turned to see Christian strolling through the door, his head held high, but he didn't look at me as he made his way back to the kitchen and pulled his pan back onto the burner.

"Thank you," I said, but he still didn't say anything, so I kept going, "I'm not going to apologize for the way I acted, Christian." He stopped what he was doing, not even flinching when the pot he held dropped onto the counter, making a loud noise, and finally turned to look at me. "I meant everything I said, and deep down, you know I was right, or you would have never done what you did. You must understand that. I appreciate what you did, truly," I insisted, but he ignored me once more, turning back to pick the pot back up.

As he worked, I stared at him, watching him ignore me, waiting for him to do something, anything, but he never did. His back was to me, tense, and his movements were swift and critical like he was doing each thing on purpose. I waited for what felt like hours, but there was nothing but the purposeful silence drowning out the clinking of utensils and sizzling of food.

I pushed myself off the couch and turned towards Christian, putting my hands behind my back as I said through rolling eyes, "I'm going to shower. Enjoy your breakfast."

I expected him to at least argue back or come after me, but once more, there was nothing. And for some reason, that just made me madder.

"Argue back," I whispered through flaring nostrils and clenched teeth. He looked back at me with wide eyes as he set down a dirty spatula.

"What?"

"Argue back!" I yelled. "You don't get the last say. I know you're mad, so come on, argue back!"

"There's nothing left to say, Scarlett. Yes, I'm mad. You act as if I don't care for my own people. I'm a king. I have to care, which means I have to make tough calls. You wouldn't understand." he asserted, turning back to grab the same spatula.

I gritted my teeth at how insolent he was being. Taking a step forward, I threw my hands up and just let what was on my mind spew from my lips, "Well, maybe I shouldn't even become your Queen at all if you're not going to show me how to understand all this. It would make this easier, no? I go back to the sectors, and you go back to being the stuck-up King I always thought you were." I was right, wasn't I? I was right for having hated him all this time.

A growl shook the room, and I stopped in my tracks and looked at him as he stalked towards me like he was the predator, and I was his prey. The worst part, though, was that I was ready.

CHAPTER TWELVE

◆◇◆

Scarlett

I gulped as he approached me with golden eyes.

"Would you like to repeat that? I'm sure my wolf would love it." he snapped.

"I said maybe I should-" I didn't get to complete my sentence because his lips were pinned to mine harshly. Instinctively, my hands laced through his hair, pulling him closer— if that was even possible. He let out a growl as I tugged harder, somewhat trying to release my anger, and his hands went from my face to my hips, where he held them tightly.

"You are mine. You are going nowhere, and you will accept your title," he demanded, panting as he pulled away from the heated kiss.

I didn't know what came over me, but I knew I might regret it later as the words left my mouth. "Show me. Show me you want me here. Show me that if I become Queen, you will consider my perspective on things, and you will listen." I pulled my hair from one side, revealing my neck to him, and he took a step back.

"You don't know what you're asking of me, Scarlett," he said, taking another step backward, but I grabbed his hand, stopping him.

"I'm asking you to mark me. Claim me as your mate. This way, I know you truly want to make this work. So I can understand what's going on through that head of yours, and I can feel your emotions and know what to do about them," I murmured, and he took a deep breath, trying to control himself.

"Please," I pleaded.

Marking your mate was an extremely intimate act, but I didn't care at the moment. One bite from him, and we could mind- link. I would feel his emotions, and I would be tied to him and him to me. We would be one.

He stepped closer and I brought his lips to mine once more. No matter how much it may hurt, it'd be worth it. Once his lips left mine, he placed a small kiss on my neck.

"Are you sure?" he asked again as I felt his breath on the nape of my neck, the spot right above my collarbone where a male marks his mate.

I nodded, tightening my hands onto his shirt. I felt his canines scraping the spot, and before I knew it, he bit down onto my shoulder. I groaned, arching my back up and tilting my neck even farther to the side. The pain was flashing through my shoulder and down to my chest. It felt as if a string was tying us together, but the pain soon ended, and I closed my eyes in relief.

I felt his canines leave, and he pulled back, grabbing a nearby cloth, and wiped the mark clean. My eyes widened, feeling my whole body responding as I saw the lustful look in his eyes.

Christian was no longer in control. His eyes were utterly golden, with no flecks of brown present.

A small growl escaped his chest as he pulled me closer to him, burying his face into my neck and taking in my scent. The one thing powerful about mates is their scents. It's a calming manner to wolves. Where flesh met flesh, sparks flew—sparks more intense than tingles—and I could feel things I had never experienced before.

The next time he pulled back, his eyes were closed. My fingers curled around his shirt, and I mumbled out his name unsurely. He took a deep breath before slowly opening his eyes. He blinked a couple of times before I noticed that his eyes were back to their original color. I felt myself smiling before he gave me a breath-taking smile of his own.

"I hate fighting with you, so I don't want to do that anymore. No more yelling at me and trying to get me mad; it will never end well when you taunt my title as King. Promise me that you won't do that again." he grumbled light-heartedly, staring down at me through long lashes.

"I promise I won't call you a stuck-up king." I joked, and he let out a small laugh.

"My Goddess..." he grumbled again.

"But thank you for sending troops to the sectors. It meant more to me than you know. Now that you know what it's like, you have to start considering other options for the sectors. You can't just forget about them. They're people too." I explained, wrapping my arms around his neck.

"I know, and I'm sorry I didn't realize that before. Maybe you were right, and maybe I wasn't a good enough king if I didn't see how bad it truly was there."

"Christian, you're a great king. I let my anger get the better of me , but you had to learn that you weren't looking at the bigger picture. Maybe the Goddess paired us together for a reason, and maybe I'm the person that needed to show you that so you *can* be the best king this country has seen."

"Maybe so, but I would also like to say that you confuse the hell out of me. One minute we're arguing and the next, I'm marking you? Confusing if you ask me." he joked.

I took in a deep breath before admitting, "I confuse myself sometimes. I just want to know you better. I want to know what you're feeling. You're so unresponsive sometimes." I rested my head against his chest.

"I see."

"Chris?"

"Hm?"

"Would I ever be able to mark you?" I asked, looking up at him as his brows furrowed some.

"Why do you ask?"

"Because I want to," I replied, but I knew the rumors about the curse of a Queen's marking.

"It's impossible for a queen to mark her king. We don't understand why, but in the past, the mark simply healed within a day. Maybe our ancestors deemed it as wrong or unmanly, but if I could... I would let you in a heartbeat." Well that sucks. "Besides, you will have your mark on me one day," he added, and I looked up at him, confused.

"How so?"

"Our wedding bands. When we mate, our scent will be mixed. When we have children, a family." My heart warmed at the thought. Does he really think about that? My wolf was crying out in joy.

Thinking about family made me think of my own. "My mom won't leave to go to the Power Pack," I finally told Chris, and his features dropped.

"Why?"

"She doesn't want to leave her friends in this mess, I guess. Poor Ashlee, what is she going to do? She can't defend herself. I've seen it with my own eyes— even felt it with my own body." I said, and he sighed.

"I understand why they would want to stay, but I can talk to them if you would like. As for Ashlee, I can have her brought here." he offered, and I shook my head.

"My parents are stubborn. They won't come until this is over, and they won't let Ashlee leave them."

We heard a knock on the door, and he let out a deep sigh.

"This is probably something you don't want to hear, but I have a meeting. All Alphas are here." I nodded in understanding, letting him go with just a little sadness.

"See you later," I mumbled, watching his retreating figure.

***

I walked around the garden, admiring the flowers. It was so beautiful out here. How could someone not love this?

Maids were here and there. It was quiet, mostly.

"Well, look what we have here."

I turned, seeing a familiar blonde and grinned. "Octavia!" I smiled, making my way to her.

"Queen Scarlett," she bowed her head in respect.

"I think we're much past formalities." I giggled. "Call me Scarlett."

"I did kind of accuse you of being a gold digger and didn't know you were the queen at the time. Sorry about that," she spoke sheepishly.

I waved a dismissive hand. "Oh, it's fine, I'm sure others have said much worse about me. What brings you to the Royal Pack?"

"It's rather shocking actually," she said, and I motioned her over to the bench.

"Spill," I chirped, smiling ear to ear. I missed girl talk. I really needed to make some friends here.

"I'm Alpha Mason's mate," she spoke barely above a whisper.

"What?" I managed to get out.

"Y-yeah." I couldn't help but notice her unhappiness about it.

"And you aren't excited?" I asked.

"How could I be? He's ruthless, Scarlett. We both have our past being a hindrance to the bond." Oh yes, I assumed she'd heard the stories about him.

"He's the Alpha of War. What else would you expect?" I asked.

"A mate. He's so cold towards me. I didn't even want to come to this today, but he didn't care. He has maybe spoken three normal words to me that wasn't commanding me around," she confessed.

I sat, shocked. "That's odd..."

"Why do you say that?" she asked.

"He was different, and I guess somewhat outgoing the last time I saw him. He even saved me from a near disaster." She stared at me, skeptically.

"Then why does he seem like he hates me, Scarlett?"

I shrugged. "I heard he's had a rough past. Maybe he knows now that since he has found his mate, he will have to share that past with someone. He was used to being closed off. Maybe this is his way of trying to avoid the situation. I don't know. You're just going to have to tear down his walls, Octavia."

"How?"

"Well, there's always seduction," I joked, and she spewed out a laugh.

"I'll get right on that."

"I'm serious, though. Try and talk to him. Get him to explain some things to you. If it goes south, just do what I do: threaten his ego." I mused, and again she laughed.

"How do I do that?"

"Say you're going to go elsewhere."

"And this works for you?" she raised a brow, and I shrugged, pulling back my hair, showing my mark.

"You could say that," I smirked, and she let out a squeal.

"He marked you! Oh, my Goddess! This is huge." I grinned widely at her glee.

"I know." I smiled, basically having a girly moment, and after a few, we calmed down.

"I'm jealous." she pouted.

"Don't be. We had a huge fight today. He keeps himself so calm and collected and won't even argue back. It makes me mad." *Geez, I sound crazy.*

"Well, he is the king after all. He's probably mastered it over the years. He's like a God to people; he has to remain calm and collected. Sometimes that's what us wolves have to look to."

"I guess you're right."

"Do you want to get out of here?" she offered, and I grinned, nodding.

"Well, I'll have to ask Christian, but I'm sure he won't mind."

***

"Absolutely not." Christian and Mason said in unison.

"What? Why not?" I whined as Octavia and I pouted. "Please?! You can send a guard with us! We just want to go to the mall." I bargained.

Christian looked down, thinking about it.

"You're not actually considering this, are you?" Mason said to Christian.

"Boys, just let the girls have fun. Don't be a party pooper." Alpha Ryker spoke, looking up to Christian with a smug grin.

"Do you want your teeth knocked out? I have no problem managing that!" Mason snapped.

"Please try," Ryker mocked, leaning his arms on the table with challenging eyes.

"I'm starting to question whether you're both nine years old? Sit down and act your age before I knock *both* of your teeth out." Alpha Jackson snapped, and let out a huff of content shortly after the two men shut up.

Ryker rolled his eyes, annoyed. "You guys aren't in the least bit scary, but please do try to intimidate me."

"Christian, please..." I begged with puppy eyes.

"Jackson, you're the smartest man here. What do you think?" Christian asked smugly as if he knew Jackson would shoot the idea down.

"Hunters are currently abroad. It will be adequate for them to go. The decision is up to you." Jackson replied, and Christian's smug look disappeared as my eyes lit up.

Ryker rolled his eyes as we all stared at Jackson. "English, please," he grumbled, fixing his cuff links to his suit.

"Hunters are more on the west side right now, migrating in the other direction. The mall would be perfectly safe if they had a guard to escort them." Jackson clarified, slowly aiming it at Ryker.

Christian sighed in defeat. "Okay, I'll send my guard, Luke, with you. I trust him."

"If anything happens, you call me immediately, alright?" Mason said to Octavia, who nodded with excitement.

"Of course."

That man cares more about her than she thinks.

CHAPTER THIRTEEN

◆◇◆

Scarlett

"**R**un, Scarlett!" Octavia yelled, having the time of her life as we ran from our clueless guard, letting out a loud laugh.

"We lied!" I said, stopping in the mall parking lot, and she grinned at me, breathless.

"Okay, so we may have climbed out the mall's restroom window, leaving our guard, but who cares?" she said, and I looked around, seeing no one and felt slightly panicked.

"Now, my friend Liza is having a party, and we're going!" she chirped.

"Oh... oh okay," I spoke, not knowing what else to say. I didn't want her to get mad at me. She's the only girlfriend I had at the moment.

Not a moment later, she grabbed my keys from my hands and smirked. "Let's go."

I'm going to die.

***

"You have got to be kidding me!" Octavia yelled, frustrated. "How could we forget to get gas out of all things?"

"I know. We're dead," I mumbled to myself, leaning against the car. I knew this was a terrible idea. "Might as well go back and deal with the wrath of our mates," I added, liking that idea better than staying out here stranded.

"Um, no? The Power Pack is maybe ten minutes down the road. I'll have Liza take us back and have someone get our car later, come on. We'll change into our dresses we bought when we get there, so grab the bags from the trunk." she ordered, and I nodded with a sigh.

As I shut the trunk, something caught onto my wolf's hearing. She barely picked it up, but it sent her into alert, sending me into alert.

"Okay, lets—" I cut Octavia off, waving my arms frantically and pointed to my ear.

She stopped and carefully moved her hair away from her ear to listen. Her eyes widened, picking it up also.

It was low breathing.

I smelled the wolfsbane before I saw it, and Octavia lunged forward, knocking me to the ground. The bullet missed, hitting the tree behind me. Not wasting a moment, Octavia pushed me under the car as she stayed out, and I looked at her like she was crazy.

"Trust me. That crap hurts. Stay down. You're my queen, I protect you, not the other way around." She whispered so low, I barely heard it.

I saw her eyes flash a yellowish gold, signaling her wolf was taking control. As if I was just going to sit here. Did she not know I was from the sectors?

"Come out! Don't be a coward!" she taunted.

Not letting her have all the fun, I rolled out from underneath the car and started looking around. Ever since Christian marked me, my eyesight and hearing were better, almost like I inherited his.

I saw the intruders as I peeked over the car. They were behind a bush, and Octavia's back was to them. She was going to get herself killed!

I stood up so quickly, rolling over the car and knocking both of us down into a ditch as another shot was fired. It wasn't the time to be thinking about how badass that was, but I did.

"Hi," I smiled while Octavia looked at me as if I were stupid, which I probably was. "Stay low," I mocked as I dove into the bushes next to me and looked around. They were nowhere to be seen, so I used my hearing.

"I'm out of bullets." It was faint but audible.

"Me too. I used too many earlier. This looks like it's going to be hand to hand," another voice said.

Hand in hand, huh? My favorite kind of fight.

"They're out of bullets," I informed Octavia.

She grinned, standing up, knowing the fight was already won. "Come on out."

Two males emerged from a brush pile within seconds, and she motioned them forward, getting into a fighting stance.

"Cute," one male said.

"She's not one to piss off," I defended, walking beside Octavia as I folded my arms. I wasn't threatened by them anymore. Not since I knew they were out of bullets. They were weak compared to us.

"Two female wolves? Do you really think you stand a chance?"

Octavia scoffed. "You hurt my feminist side," she joked, placing a hand over her heart.

"Typical women. Are you going to go cry to your boyfriends now?"

We looked at each other, already annoyed and pissed off. We gave each other a quick nod before launching ourselves at them. One man swung at me, but I ducked, quickly knocking his legs out from underneath him, dropping him onto the ground. Before he could get up, I sat my heel on his neck, waiting to plunge it through. I stared down at the fearful man with a smug look.

I looked over to Octavia as she had the other man already on his knees. She growled, delivering a kick so hard he flew into the tree behind him.

"Didn't you hear? Wolves rule hunters drool. How's *that* for being a woman?" she snorted, stalking towards the man, kicking him onto his back and placing her foot on his neck like I did.

"Sleep tight," she grinned, raising her foot, knocking him out cold with a kick.

I looked down at the guy underneath the sharp heel of my shoe. "Ever wondered what happens when a heel gets stabbed through someone's jugular?" I asked him.

"N-no," he stuttered out.

"Try what you did again, and you will." I turned to Octavia. "Octavia, would you like to do the honors?" I asked.

"Would love to," she grinned once more, sauntering over, knocking another man out cold with a simple kick.

"Let's tie them up and put them in the trunk. We have a party to get to," she grinned, looking as if she was invincible.

This girl will be the death of me.

We eventually arrived at the party, and I felt as if I were about to throw up. I walked side by side with Octavia nervously. *It was huge.* My phone had died on the way here, which only added to the long list of deep trouble I was in. Octavia was quick to make us change and head out to meet her friend.

"Liza!" Octavia squealed to a girl with straight black hair. She was gorgeous.

"Tav! Who's this?" Liza asked as she looked at me and I smiled.

"This is my new and best friend, Scarlett. Look, we have to keep eyes on her. She's a golden prize. Anything happens to her, and we're dead."

"Hey!" I protested, but Octavia only laughed and shot me a wink.

"Wait, Scarlett...as in..?"

"She's the King's mate!" Octavia shouted over the music.

Given the knowledge, Liza's eyes widened, and she quickly bowed her head. "I'm so sorry, your majesty. Please let me know if you need anything." Liza said as I rolled my eyes playfully.

"Please, just call me Scarlett. No formal introductions necessary. Just think of me as one of you girls!"

"I'd be honored!" she grinned hugely at me and linked each of her arms with one of ours.

"Where have you been lately?" Liza asked Octavia.

"Uh, she's been crashing with me for a while. I met her at the ball and just wanted to get to know her. Make a new friend, you know?" I covered while Octavia shot me a thankful look.

"Oh! Understandable!" We stopped in front of a bar as Liza let us go and grabbed two cups before handing them to us.

"Is this...?" Octavia started to ask, and Liza grinned, nodding.

"It's just a tiny bit of wolf's venom and tequila."

Wow. Wolf's venom was a potent drink for wolves. It was the only thing that got us super hammered.

"Sounds good to me," Octavia said, chugging it down.

Yep, she is literally insane.

"Warning... The barbie squad is here," Liza whispered, and I gave her a confused look.

"There is this group of girls from our college that come to these types of parties. Cassidy Lockwood, Marty Heathers, Madison Kepner, and Lisa Rivers. They're all over there with their ugly attitudes." informed Octavia, pointing to a group of people.

They did look vicious. I even felt threatened when one caught my gaze and flashed me a dirty look.

"Let's dance!" Octavia said, pulling me to the dance floor as Liza went to speak to some other friends of hers that had just entered.

Nervously, I followed her onto the dance floor. She instantly let loose, dancing happily. Joining along, we were soon laughing and having fun, something I hadn't done in a long time. I took a bold move and took a sip of my drink and cringed. *It was horrible.*

"Woo!" Octavia called out, and I laughed at her as she acted silly, dancing, already feeling the wolf's venom's buzz.

I was moving my hips to the song's rhythm when I felt two hands grasp my waist. Quickly, I pulled away, staring wide-eyed at a guy I didn't even know.

"Derek, go somewhere else. You're not wanted here." Octavia was quick to shoo him away.

"I was just trying to have some fun. Come on," he fake pouted as he took a step towards me while I took a step backward but knocked into someone.

The music was cut off when I heard a scream. Turning around, I saw one of the girls I was previously warned about covered in her drink. I quickly sat my drink on a chair next to me and held my hands up.

"You idiot!" she screamed at me.

"I'm sorry, I didn't mean to." I apologized truthfully, and she rolled her eyes.

"You totally did. I saw you looking at me earlier. You're just jealous of me," she sneered, and I was taken aback.

"Look, I was just trying to be nice by apologizing, but you're making it harder. Let's get one thing straight, I am not, in any way, jealous of you. How about you stop making up lies and treating everyone around you like complete garbage and get a better personality?"

"Y-you homewrecker!" I rolled my eyes at the pathetic comeback.

"Quite the opposite," I snorted, and she let out a sound between a scream and a growl and turned, pushing her way through the crowd.

"You owe her a new dress," one of her groupies said, and I rolled my eyes.

"I owe her nothing." I turned to make my way to Octavia, but that Derek guy stepped in my way again.

"Move!" I was fed up and just wanted to go home to my mate—that was probably going to kill me.

"What you did wasn't cool. That was my sister!" he snapped.

I crossed my arms. "Oh yeah? What are you going to do about it, big guy? Hit me?" Gasps were heard around the room as he clenched his jaw.

"Derek! I'm warning you, get away from her for your own good." I heard Octavia call out, but one of his goons held her back.

"Derek!" Liza joined in. "She's a royal— the Queen! You will be slaughtered," Liza continued, and more gasps sounded throughout the room as whispers broke out.

Once again, I tried to move past him, but he pushed me by my shoulders with a great force, and I went flying to the ground, hitting it with a thump.

Ow.

"Stop! Please!" Liza screamed.

Any wolf seeing their Queen in distress shook them up. Hell, her being in distress made *me* shaken up.

"I don't care if she's a damn royal. They're all stuck up anyways. It'll be good for you to be shown your place for once in a while." His eyes shifted to his wolf's color, and my eyes widened. *This guy was crazy.*

He took a step towards me, but soon stopped when a thunderous growl shook the whole house.

I directed my attention to the front doors, and sure enough, all alpha's stood with fire in their eyes. Derek noticeably gulped as Christian took large steps towards us.

"Anyone leaves this house, and I will hold you in the pack cells for Goddess knows how long!" Alpha Ryker yelled to the people of his pack, and everyone froze. The cells of any pack were known for being terrifying.

Mason walked behind Christian as they made their way to us, and Mason's eyes shifted to a threatening red as he walked with authority towards the goons holding his mate.

Christian instantly had Derek by the collar, pulling him towards himself so they were face to face. "How dare you lay your hands not only on my pack member, someone who is above you, but on your Queen," he growled.

Chris drew his arm back, delivering a punch so hard I saw blood fly from Derek's mouth. Shrieks erupted from nearby girls as everyone stood paralyzed in fear. Mason growled at the two boys who held Octavia, instantly making them release her. As soon as she was free, she ran into his arms without even thinking about it. The best part, though, was how he held her so tightly and close to him.

"I was worried," he mumbled, and my heart fluttered for them.

Christian pulled me to him and looked me over.

"I'm fine," I mumbled.

"You teens need to check yourselves! You didn't even notice you were in a room with your soon to be Queen! Then, you let her get hands laid on her by a man! Only *two* girls stepped up to fight for her. You should be ashamed!" Alpha Jackson called out.

"She may be my mate, and she may be your Queen, but you let a woman get pushed around by a man. You shouldn't have let the two get at each other's throats, to begin with! Do you have no respect for either party here? I trust you will take this as a lesson. I will personally see to it that every one of you is punished." Christian declared, pulling me to his side tightly.

Great, now people were going to hate me. This night, in general, was horrible.

"And I will personally see to it that it happens. I am ashamed of you all! This is the Power Pack! We don't have a reputation for hitting women nor starting unnecessary fights. Come on now! I, as your alpha, feel so disrespected. You let our queen be in harm's way! Get your head out of your phones and narcissistic asses and into the news. Maybe that way, you can see who is and isn't your damn queen." I felt happy hearing Alpha Ryker's speech. I think that was the first time I saw him act seriously.

"I don't know about most here, but I was raised to never lay my hand on a woman no matter the circumstances. Especially if I didn't even have a damn good reason for doing it. I know Scarlett can take care of herself and probably would have taken your pal, Derek, here down too, but it is up to us men to respect the women around us." Mason growled out.

"As of tonight, I, Alpha Ryker, banish you, Derek Merrington, from my pack. You are stripped of being a Power Pack member." Ryker declared, and Derek cried out in pain.

Getting stripped and banished from a pack is painful. It severs any ties you once had.

"I, King Christian, declare you, Derek Merrington, as a rogue." Derek cried out in even more pain, but it wasn't over yet. We still had another alpha.

"I, Alpha Mason, declare you, Derek Merrington, a prisoner of the War Pack for threatening the queen, which is against one of our most sacred laws. Respect the royals and respect your Queen and King. Your sentence will be determined once we make our way back to my pack. May the Goddess be with you." The small banishing ritual was over, and Alpha Jackson shook his head.

"I, Alpha Jackson, declare you stupid." he mocked, and I had to bite my tongue to hold in my laugh… he just had to get the last word in.

"Pack police are on their way. I have notified all parents, which are quite a few. We shall see who gets themselves beat tonight." Ryker said, grinning, and Christian and Mason were already pulling Octavia and me to an exit.

"Don't think either of you are off the hook yet," Christian growled out, and me and Octavia looked at each other in fear, knowing we were in for an ear full.

CHAPTER FOURTEEN

$\leftarrow\diamond\rightarrow$

Scarlett

S cared was an understatement. *I was terrified.* I had never seen
Christian this mad before. Alpha Mason being here didn't help
it either.

When we entered Christian's office, they pushed us towards the
couch, and we both sat practically holding onto each other. The drive
over was so quiet I was afraid to breathe too loud.

"I cannot even begin to describe how angry I am," Christian said,
folding his arms and leaning against the front of his desk.

"You don't have to. It's okay," Octavia spoke barely above a whisper.

"No smart remarks while we're talking either," Mason snapped,
sending a glare to Octavia. "What made you lie to us? Was it something
we did?"

"We were sick of doing nothing all the time! I love spending time with
you, Christian, but sometimes I'm going to want to spend time with my

friends. I want to go to places and stop staring at the walls of this palace. I know what we did was stupid and childish, but sometimes you have to let me breathe," I confessed, and he sighed, pinching the bridge of his nose.

"*Let you breathe?* I'm sorry that we're in the middle of a war and I can't let you go party and get drunk with your so-called 'friends'. It's not safe! You're about to be Queen, Scarlett. Do you know what this could do to your reputation?!"

"Nothing's safe anymore! As far as my reputation goes, I don't care. I'm not going to be some Queen stuck in this palace fearing the unknown and letting you do everything while I sit idly by." I gritted out.

"You could've gotten hurt. Hell, you almost did! Be grateful I was there in time," he snapped, and I rolled my eyes.

"Please, I could have handled him just. Just like I handled that hunter." but as soon as those words left my mouth, I felt Octavia's grip tighten around my arm.

Oh no.

"What did you just say?" Mason gritted out.

"Mason! Did I ever tell you how great your new haircut lo—"

"Answer me, *now.*" he cut me off, and I closed my eyes in defeat.

"We may or may not have run out of gas, so we decided to walk to the Power Pack. Then hunters showed up. They're currently tied up inside our trunk," I mumbled, wanting this to be over as quickly as possible.

"I cannot believe this!" Christian said, standing up, looking exasperated.

"Whose idea was this?" Mason asked.

"Mine," Octavia confessed. "Though, if that guard weren't with us in the first place, then maybe we would have stayed and wouldn't have felt the need to go against the rules," she added.

"Would you really have stayed?" Mason asked.

"Probably not... but it's the thought that counts," she replied with a snarky tone, adding more fuel to the flame.

"This...*this* is why I never wanted a mate! I don't want to have to babysit someone! If you die, I die! So, now I'm going to have to worry you're not trying to do something stupid constantly. You're an immature teen, Octavia! Grow up. I don't even know why the Goddess paired me with you." Mason finally snapped, letting all his built-up anger out, and I let out a loud growl.

"Hey! Back off!" I snarled as I saw Octavia look down with tear-filled eyes. "And here I was telling her you were such a great guy, Mason, but I was wrong. You're a jerk."

"Scarlett, watch your tone. He is an alpha." Christian scolded.

"What, Christian? Are you going to say you practically hate your mate too?" I asked, agitated, standing up and pulling Octavia up with me. "I honestly don't want to hear anything else you two have to say right now. I understand that we messed up and that you're angry, but I draw the line when you come after my friend and make her cry." I calmly replied, pulling Octavia towards the doors.

"Where do you think you two are going? We're not done talking!" Mason snarled, taking a step towards us.

"I don't want to disrespect you, Mason, but I'm not exactly calm at the moment myself. Let us go, and we can all talk when we've all collected ourselves. If there's one thing that you need to know about me, it's that I stand up for the ones I care about, no matter the situation."

I thought my words over before I continued. "What you said to your mate was hurtful, and I think you really need to dwell on that before she comes back to you with a rejection of the mate bond." Christian's eyes widened at my comment, and Mason slowly looked at Octavia, his features softening as realization sat in.

"Come on. Let's just go." Octavia mumbled softly.

***

"I hate having a mate," Octavia sobbed, taking a bite of her ice cream.

"He'll come around," I reassured her, but she only shook her head.

"No, he won't. He's a jerk who only cares about himself. Maybe what you said was right, maybe I should just reject the bond and move on with my life."

"What I saw tonight when he took you from those goons was anything but that. He cares, whether he wants to show it or not, he cares." I told her softly.

"You really think that?" I nodded, and she sighed, sitting the tub of ice cream on the coffee table.

"I miss my mom." she sniffled, laying across my lap, and I pulled her to me, playing with her hair.

"Me too." I let out a small laugh at the thought of her. "She would have probably beaten Mason with a flip flop if she heard him say that." Octavia couldn't help but laugh.

"Could you call her for me?"

I let out a laugh, nodding. "When I was in the sectors, there was this boy that would always tease my sister and me. My mom saw it one day and waved her finger at him, saying 'Asi es como se debe tratar a una dama' and the boy just ran away. A calm Latina is a scary Latina." I replied, and Octavia looked up at me.

"What does that mean?"

"That's not how you treat a lady." She smiled at my reply, nodding.

"You have a smart mother." I nodded in agreement and suddenly realized just how much I missed my mom.

After a minute, she sighed. "Do you think they hate us?"

"I don't think so. They're just upset that we did something so childish. As much as I hate to admit it, we knew we were doing something wrong, yet we did it anyway. I'm the soon-to-be queen. I can't be seen out partying and getting into fights. None of this is their fault. It's ours, and we need to take responsibility for that. What Mason said, though, was hurtful and out of line, so I'm not excusing his behavior, but we know who's really in the wrong here."

She nodded and looked back down. "I know, but I'm not ready to face Mason just yet. I'm just going to go to my room and pray he isn't there."

I nodded, looking at the time, seeing it was two in the morning. "Good luck, maybe he's still with Christian."

She gave me a small laugh. "I sure hope so."

***

When I stepped out of the shower and wrapped a towel around me, Christian's scent slowly invaded my senses. Trying to be quick, I changed into some clothes I'd brought in with me. I opened the bathroom door, and sure enough, Christian was sitting at the end of the bed with his head cast down, his arms resting on his thighs. When he noticed my presence, he slowly looked up at me with tired eyes.

"I'm sorry," he apologized.

"You have nothing to apologize over. It's me who should be apologizing. I acted childish and stubborn back there." I mumbled, and he opened his arms for me. I happily walked over to him as he pulled me onto his lap, wrapping me in his embrace.

"I was just so worried. I nearly killed the guard when he told me you were nowhere to be found."

"I'm sorry. I just… actually, I don't know what happened. It was a spur of the moment decision. What you did for me at that party, though, you stood up for me, so thank you. It meant a lot to me." He gave me a small smile before leaning in, capturing my lips with his.

"Anything for you," he mumbled against them.

He pulled back, running his thumb over my cheek, and I leaned into his touch. "I'm sorry for being such a brat, though, I really am. I just can't believe Mason said those things to Octavia, Christian. I could never imagine you saying something like that to me." I shook my head at the painful thought.

"Honestly, I was shocked too, but I think what you said to him snapped him into reality. She could have easily rejected him tonight for the way he was acting towards her, but she didn't." he looked me in the eyes, a nervous look on his face. "You would never reject me, would you?"

"Never," I smiled, leaning in to place a soft kiss on his lips. "I may like to argue, but I know when I'm in the wrong." I joked, and he belched out a laugh.

"You sure do. Goddess, I don't think I can take any more arguments between us." I giggled at his response, leaning my head against his chest.

"Also, the hunters in your trunk have been dealt with." he informed me, and I remained silent, not really wanting to know their fate.

After a few minutes of silence, I spoke, "Christian?"

"Hm?"

"I think I'm falling in love with you, and I'm terrified," I confessed, and I felt him place a kiss on the top of my head.

"Me too, Scarlett, me too."

CHAPTER FIFTEEN

$\diamond$

Scarlett

The next morning, I woke up to Christian getting ready for an early meeting. Knowing that he would be gone for a while, I decided to get up and go for a run, as my wolf hadn't been let out in a while.

As minutes passed, I found myself lying in a field still in wolf form. She was happy and content, feeling free. I know some royal guards were trailing me, but I didn't care. It felt terrific being outside, and it was a beautiful day. The field was full of fresh flowers, and I kept taking in the unique scents, happy just to be feeling free again.

Hours passed of me just lying there. I thought about everything; the war, my old friends, my family.

"Where are you?" a mind-link ran through, and I immediately noticed it was Christian.

"Went out for a run. I thought I told you?" I answered.

"You did. I'm just asking where you're at."

'Oh, I'm in the field by the old pack houses. It's beautiful up here.'
I got no response as my wolf yawned, wanting to give me back control, but I stayed in wolf form since I was nowhere near my clothes.

As I sat thinking about how amazing it was that I could mind-link with Christian since our marking, I heard a low growl and felt as though my heart stopped for a split second. My wolf piped up, instantly taking control back, her ears alert. The guards were gone, and I started to panic. I stood looking around, but I didn't see anything. I could have sworn I—

I let out a yelp as I was tackled from the side. We rolled until I was on my back, and a paw sat on my chest, holding me down. The huge wolf looked down at me, but the gold eyes gave him away.

"Chris, what the hell!" I snapped through our link, growling at him.

"Miss me, gorgeous?" His eyes gave away his happiness.

"Not really." I lied.

He growled, snapping at my neck playfully.

Although his wolf form was intimidating, it was also beautiful. His fur was golden brown, and his size made me seem like an ant compared to him.

"Your wolf is gorgeous," he spoke, and I tilted my head to the side.

"Funny, I was thinking the same thing." I rolled out from under him and stood as he nuzzled his head with mine.

"You never told me her fur was grey, and her eyes were blue. I would have thought they were brown like yours."

I shrugged. **"You never asked, plus I don't know why. I guess she's special,"** I joked, playfully knocking his body with mine as we walked.

"I would have to agree with that."

I got an idea and mentally smirked. Nipping at his ear, I jumped back, wagging my tail and took off through the field. His chuckle drifted through our link as if saying 'game on,' so I ran like my life depended on it. He was purposely letting me ahead of him, nipping at my back legs here and there.

As I was running, I saw a small but decent-sized river and ran, jumping into it. The loud splash after me indicated Chris did too.

I came up for air and looked down at the rippling water around me. It was pretty dark, so I shifted back into my human form, trusting Christian to keep his distance. He did as I did, and I saw his handsome self again.

"Why so far away?" he teased with a small, knowing smirk.

"I'm trusting you to keep your distance." I replied, and he sighed.

"I will, only if you want."

I rolled my eyes. "I do."

He nodded, and I grinned, splashing him with water.

"Oh, you want to play that game?" he asked, and my eyes widened.

"Why do you look like you're about to kill me?" I asked, and he just grinned.

He was about to splash me back when we both froze. I heard paws hitting the ground, and in seconds Christian was beside me, pulling me to his chest and maneuvered us to where his back was facing whoever was coming. The paws stopped and I heard bones break from the shifting.

"Y-your majesty," we heard, and Christian let out a low growl.

"What?" he snapped.

How is he so calm when we're this close? He had officially invaded my trust bubble.

Wait.

Oh, my Goddess. My cheeks heated as I realized we were chest to chest with no clothes between us.

"It's important, sir. Your mother is back from her trip."

Ah, so that's where his mom has been.

"And?" Chris asked.

"And she has requested you for dinner immediately. You and Amanda." My breathing hitched. Amanda?

"Leave." We heard him retreating and I pushed Christian away, covering myself up.

"Why does your mother want to see you and Amanda?" I asked, and Christian clenched his jaw, looking straight ahead.

"Mother doesn't know about you yet," he said, and I stared agape at him.

"What do you mean, 'she doesn't know about me,' Christian?"

"She's been on a trip. What was I supposed to do? Shoot her a text saying, 'Hey mom! I met my mate today. By the way, I kicked Amanda out, and she isn't taking the throne. Love you!'"

I nodded frantically. "Obviously!" I shot back, and he sighed, rolling his eyes.

"Come on, we need to go back for dinner," he stated, and I wanted to protest, but I refrained, noticing the dark look in his eyes. He didn't seem to have a good relationship with his mother.

***

The scratching of utensils on plates was all that was heard. You could say his mom, Rebecca, didn't take the fact I was his mate well. I recall her saying something about 'people from sectors shouldn't be a queen,' but I don't remember the rest because I was too busy *mentally stabbing her with my fork.*

"So, Scarlett, what do you do?" she asked, putting a piece of steak into her mouth.

"Uh, like occupation wise?" I asked.

"Obviously."

I gripped my fork tightly. "Well, before I met Christian, I cleaned houses around the Intelligence Pack," I said, and she cocked an eyebrow, looking at Christian.

"You want your queen to be an old maid?"

I looked down, forcing back a growl.

"I would much rather it be that than a gold digger." My head quickly rose to look at Christian with wide eyes as he sat there calmly. *My mother would have beat me with her shoe for saying that!*

"Christian Dimitri Spur," his mom snapped fiercely, and he just smiled at her.

"Remember, mother, you're in my kingdom," he snapped, and I could see the gold start to flake in his eyes.

She noticeably gulped. "I just don't know why you want a sector as queen. Amanda was perf-"

I had enough.

"What is so wrong with being from a sector? Is it wrong to be a hardworking individual? If so, I am sorry. You can sit there and say whatever you want about me, but it will not change the fact that I am your son's mate. You're going to have to get over it. I will be a great queen, thank you very much, and I am going to, oh so much, love proving you wrong." I stood up, dropping my napkin onto the table, and staring at his puzzled mother. "Now, if you'll excuse me." I took off towards the doors, towards the main foyer with a triumphant look.

CHAPTER SIXTEEN

$$\text{———}\blacklozenge\text{———}$$

Christian

Watching my mate leave in a distressed manner completely pissed me off and my wolf, which was never a good combination.

"Are you serious, mother?" I asked, and she ignored me, cutting into her steak.

I slammed my fist onto the table, letting out a snarl, causing her to jump and look at me with wide eyes.

"You may be my mother, you may have been a queen, but *I* am the King now. My wolf doesn't take your actions tonight on a good measure, so I suggest you not piss him off anymore."

She sighed, bringing her napkin to her mouth.

I'd never had a good relationship with my mother. The lies she and my father kept from me when I was growing up were too much.

"I am serious, Christian. She doesn't need to be a queen! You don't know the torment she will go through, the hate. The sectors are something that can make or break you. That side of her, what she has been through, will never leave her. The pain and suffering she has endured; you wouldn't begin to understand. That takes a toll on a person. She is not fit to be queen. She won't do what's necessary, and she will pity the weak. Mate or not, I do not accept. I'm happy for you, Christian. I really am, but you have to consider everything."

I looked at her in confusion. "Consider what exactly? There is nothing to consider. I love that woman with everything in me. I'm not letting her go, ever. I've known her for a short amount of time, and it's the happiest I've ever been. She will make a great Luna and queen. Dad even agrees. I try, and I try, but you push everyone away. I see why Dad is never around now," I snapped, standing up.

"Don't try to act like you know your father better than me. You hate me from keeping things from you, and I'm sorry, but some things are better left unsaid. You wouldn't begin to understand..." she trailed off, shaking her head.

"Do not try to use his own mistakes to cover up your own. She is staying, and that is final. You know nothing about her! You've been home for an hour, and you're already trying to judge her. Listen and listen closely. I will marry Scarlett. Afterward, I will crown her as my queen, and we'll start a family. Now, it's up for you to decide whether you want to see your future daughter-in-law walk down the aisle or meet our kids. I've said what has needed to be said. Until you accept this, don't bother coming into the palace."

Her eyes narrowed as if she was waiting for me to apologize or take it back, but I stood my ground, my eyes not leaving hers. Finally, she stood up and threw her napkin onto the table.

"Not on my watch," she growled out, marching out of the dining hall.

I watched her retreating figure with anger coursing through my body. What was she up to?

Scarlett

I sat by the window that was in mine and Christian's bedroom. The sun was slowly starting to leave the sky as I wiped the tears from my eyes. I tried to act bravely in there, but the second I got back to our room, I was a goner.

I couldn't understand why Rebecca had judged me so harshly. I'd never done anything to her! So, what if I was from a sector? I may not have been her definition of perfect, but I was a good woman, and I'd be that good to Chris. Lately, I'd noticed how Christian had become my life. Anything reminded me of him. It was incredible how not too long ago I didn't even believe in mates, and here I sat patronized by his mother.

How fun.

The door creaked open, and I turned to see Christian. He gave me a soft smile, walking over to me.

"Have you been crying?" he asked.

"No," I tried to lie, but my voice gave it away.

"Oh babe, come here," he said as he pulled me up from my chair, taking my spot and pulling me back onto his lap, where I laid my head against his chest.

"Don't listen to her. She's always been a royal pain in the ass."

I let out a small laugh, sniffling. "You don't say..."

His chest vibrated with laughter.

"Why does she hate me?" I asked.

"She doesn't hate you, Scar. She's just... not easily accepting," he said, and I looked up at him.

"You once told me that you didn't have a good relationship with your father. Is it the same way with your mother?"

"Yes." I could tell he didn't want to talk about it, but he continued, nonetheless. "My father cheated on her. It was a long time ago, but because of it, I had another sister I never met, which they kept from me for years."

My jaw dropped.

"He got someone else pregnant?! You have another sister?"

"Had. She was killed. When I found out, it crushed me. Not only was he a cheater, but he let a child of his get killed, and he played a part in it."

"What? How?"

He looked out the window. "He was a king with a reputation to uphold. Being a cheater and a neglectful father isn't exactly what a king wants to be known for."

"How did you find out about all this?"

"Let's just say he let it slip one day. It's a long story with a lot of other details, but that's the short version."

"What was her name?"

"Amara."

My heart broke as I saw the hurt in his eyes at the mention of her name. He wished he could have met her, and because of his father, he'd never got that chance.

"Anyways… my mother left. I think she didn't take you nor me putting her in her place lightly." he tried to joke.

"Is this going to be bad for our relationship? She's your mother, after all." I looked down, not really wanting to know the answer.

"Honestly? I don't know. The look she had in her eyes when she left, it was like she was up to nothing good." Fear immediately filled me, and my eyes snapped to meet his.

"Is she capable of keeping us apart? W-we're mates. She can't keep us apart. Christian, I can't lose you. I don't want—"

"Shh, Scarlett, calm down, it's going to be alright. I'm the king; after all, she has no say." I nodded, somewhat relieved from his response.

What was that woman up to?

"Do you want to watch a movie or something?" he offered, and I smiled, getting up from his lap.

"A movie and popcorn?" I suggested and he let out a small laugh.

"Sounds like a plan. You pick the movie, and I'll make the popcorn."

"Aye aye, captain." I winked, spinning on my heels to where Christian stashed all his DVDs.

As I skimmed through his impressive collection, I heard my phone ring. I grabbed it off the counter and walked back to the movies after placing it to my ear.

"Hello?"

"Scarlett!" my sister's voice rang through the speaker.

"Yes? What's wrong?!" I dropped the disks and held my phone tightly in a panic.

"There's this guy and I really like him, but I don't know what to do." relief washed over me, causing me to sit down and let out a breath I didn't know I had been holding.

"Goddess, Ashlee, you nearly gave me a heart attack."

"Sorry," she mumbled sheepishly.

"Now this boy, who is he? Have I met him before?"

"Um, no… he's a royal guard, and I think he's my mate." she chirped, and I quickly sat up, eyes wide.

"Mate?! Are you sure? Did the word leave your mouth when you all saw each other?" I asked, trying to put into words how my first interaction with Christian went.

"No, but every time I see him, I get these goosebumps, and he has this scent that makes my wolf go crazy. That's how it was for you and Christian, right?"

"Yeah, kind of…" I mumbled, my heart beating furiously.

"You're only sixteen… I didn't even know that was possible, Ashlee."

"Did you ever listen to anything mom told us? When you turn sixteen, that's when you're able to notice who your mate is! He only looks to be about twenty or so."

"Twenty?!" I screeched, standing up from my chair and starting pacing.

"Scarlett, I turn seventeen in a week, it's not that big of a deal. Plus, I think he's my mate. If that's the case, then I have no problem with age."

I shook my head, running my hand over my face. "Has he said anything to you?"

"No, we have yet to exchange words, but tomorrow I'm going to try. Then I'll really know." I could practically see her beaming.

"Just… be careful, alright?"

She let out a snort, "Yeah, yeah… well, mom is home. I've got to go, I'm supposed to be cleaning the house." the line went dead, and I sighed, tossing my phone onto the couch.

"I got popcorn!" I heard and jumped, seeing Christian walk into the room.

"Everything okay?" he asked, noticing my panicked state.

"I just had the oddest phone call with my sister."

"Yeah? About what?"

"Apparently, she thinks she has found her mate."

"Mate? Oh, wow."

"Is that even possible?" I asked, and he thought about it for a second.

"Yeah, she's sixteen, right? That's when you're able to notice who your mate is ." he shrugged as if it was no big deal and popped some popcorn into his mouth.

"She thinks he's one of your guards and he 'looks about twenty'" I quoted.

He froze as he heard the words. "Oh…"

"Yeah… I hope she just doesn't get her hopes up." I sighed. "This is just another reason why they need to move into the Power Pack."

"You know that we can't make them do anything they don't want to, Scarlett." Christian reminded me gently.

"I know, I know. She's just my little sister."

Christian smiled. "She's getting older. You can't be protective over her forever."

"Oh, yes, I can." I scoffed, folding my arms, and he belched out a laugh.

"You're too cute, now come on. Let's watch this movie."

CHAPTER SEVENTEEN

◆—◇—◆

Scarlett

"No," Christian said, not looking up from his papers, and I groaned.

"Christian," I drew out as I laid on the couch in his office. "You're not going to the mall. That's final." I watched as he scribbled something— most likely his signature— onto a piece of paper and pushed it to the side before starting on another one.

"But-" I stopped talking when a low rumble escaped his chest. "Don't you growl at me, mister." I taunted as he finally looked up at me.

"Must I remind you what happened last time?" he asked, and I scoffed, folding my arms.

"No. Whenever you get any chance, you bring it up anyways. I know. I went to the mall, left my guard, and went to a party when we were in a war. Yada yada yada..."

"You act as if it wasn't a big deal, Scarlett."

"I never said it wasn't."

He rolled his eyes, turning his attention back to writing.

"How about you take me? We've never done one thing a couple would do. All you do is sit in here, writing papers and barking orders at people."

"I'm a king. It's what we do," was his only response.

Minutes went by, and I found myself sitting upside down on the couch. The blood was rushing to my head, so I tried to sit up quickly, but me being me, I embarrassingly toppled to the floor. I sat up quickly, pushing the hair out of my face and met Christian's annoyed eyes and gave him a nervous smile.

"Get your coat," he said, standing up.

"Where are we going?" I asked as he approached me and held his hand out to help me up.

"Well, since you're going to sit here and bug me all day, I might as well let you go out. I only trust you with me, though, so this is what you get," he smirked at me, but I couldn't care less. I was just happy I got to do something outside the palace!

"Yes!" I squealed like a child, and he shook his head, amused.

"Well, go on then," he motioned for me to go through the door I was blocking, and I grinned.

"Let me change!" I said and was about to walk off when he grabbed my arm.

"What's wrong with what you have on? You look fine."

"Christian, I'm going outside of the palace. Sweatpants aren't going to cut it. I need to look good."

"For who?" he asked warily.

"Myself, you big oaf," I teased, and he squinted his eyes at my nickname. "Ha," I laughed nervously and darted down the hall.

***

"Why do you have so many cars?" I asked as we walked through his huge garage full of them.

"You like to argue, I like to have cars." he winked, causing me to roll my eyes.

"Yeah, but what I like to do doesn't cost me one hundred thousand to do so."

He just laughed as we stopped in front of a beautiful black car. "What even is this?" I asked, looking it over, and he snickered at my baffled expression.

"You don't know cars?"

I raised an amused eyebrow at him. "Honey, does it look like I know what type of car this is? I couldn't tell you one car name. I walked everywhere in the sectors."

"Right…" He looked caught off guard by my comment but cleared his throat.

"It's an Aston Martin."

I didn't even know what that was, but it sounded expensive and sure looked it.

"Do you know anything about cars in general?" he asked as he opened the door for me, and I slid in.

"Not really, I just know the basics," I answered, and he looked deep in thought, but closed the door and walked around to get in as well.

"So, I'm assuming you were never taught to drive?"

Once again, I shook my head. "Nope."

"Want me to teach you one day?"

I smiled at his offer. "Sure." We pulled on our seatbelt, and seconds later, the engine roared to life as he started it and sped out of the garage and down the driveway.

"Woo!" I chirped, feeling as if I should throw my hands up in the air.

As he grinned over at me, then directed his attention back to the road, I knew I wasn't the only one enjoying our trip out.

"So, where are we going? Nowhere too crazy, I suppose, considering our lapdogs trailing us." I mused, watching two black SUVs following behind us.

"We have to have guards, you know this, but are you hungry?"

"I could eat."

"How does Italian sound?" he asked.

"Sounds pretty good, looks even better," I grinned up at him, waiting for him to catch my joke.

"Do you want me to stop this car?" he asked, looking over at me, and I let out a loud laugh.

"No." *Maybe.*

"Then, no teasing."

I just nodded, biting back my smile.

Christian had put on some music as we drove, and I loved every second of it.

It didn't take long until we pulled up at a fancy restaurant. "Wait here," he ordered, getting out of the car.

Confused, I watched him get out and walk to the other side of the car. My door opened, and he smiled at me as he held his hand out. I just laughed, unbuckling my seatbelt, and grabbed it, stepping out.

"I will always open the door for you, so you might as well just wait."

"How sweet," I teased, and he just smiled, lacing our fingers together as he locked the car, and we walked to the doors.

"Right this way, your majesties." a lady said, and I looked up at him, squinting my eyes.

"You own this, don't you?"

He just smirked, continuing to walk.

Of course, he did.

We took our booth in a secluded area in the restaurant, and my eyes nearly popped out when I looked at the menu's prices.

"Twenty dollars for a salad?!"

He chuckled, nodding. "Good quality food."

"Is the lettuce gold or something?" I exaggerated.

"Totally. The leaves shine with every bite." he played along, causing me to let out a small laugh.

"What's good here?" I asked.

"I like different things," he said, looking it over.

"What's your favorite Italian food?"

"That's tough. Honestly, I'll eat any type of pasta. What about you?"

"Uh, I'm basic mainly because I've only ever had fettuccine."

"Alfredo, correct?"

Isn't there only one type?

"I thought that was the only one."

He belched out a laugh, causing me to smile. He looked so carefree. "Fettuccine is the noodle, babe. There are many sauces you can do with it."

"Oh." My cheeks heated and he laughed softly.

A waitress came to our table and gave us a huge smile.

"What can I get you?" she asked.

He smiled at the waitress, speaking something in I'm assuming Italian. I don't know how the waitress didn't swoon right there.

"Sì, naturalmente." she responded as I stared at her agape.

Does everyone here know Italian?

Christian looked at me. "Do you like shrimp?"

"Yeah…"

"Go ahead and bring us the Tuscan shrimp penne." he told her.

"Of course, sir." She walked away and I looked at him.

"What if I didn't want that?"

"Would you like me to call her back here? I just figured you may want to try something new. I'm sorry."

"It's fine," I waved him off. "Honestly, I couldn't read the menu besides the prices. What were you two talking about in Italian?"

"She asked what we wanted, then I told her to get us some wine."

"Can you teach me? I mean just the basics."

He looked surprised by my question, but slowly smiled, nodding. "I'd love to, but only if you teach me some Spanish."

I grinned. "I think I can do that."

His phone started ringing, but instead of answering, he hit the lock button, ignoring it. *I wasn't complaining.*

"So, tell me more about yourself." Christian smiled, folding his hands together.

"What do you want to know?" I asked as the waitress came back, pouring us some wine.

"Favorite color?"

"Purple," I smiled.

"Favorite movie?"

"*Twilight*." He scoffed at the response.

"Kidding, I'm only kidding. Probably twenty-one Jump Street." he shook his head at me, a small smile on his face.

"Favorite...food, in general?"

I thought about it. "Definitely cheese sticks."

He laughed. "Out of all the food there is, that is your favorite?"

"Any time my mother had extra money, she would always surprise me with them. It's silly, but it was nice of her."

"That is nice of her. She seems like a great woman."

"She is. My turn!" I said, but he shook his head.

"Nope, not done."

I rolled my eyes, sitting back in my chair.

"When you were little, what did you want to be when you were older?"

I covered my face, embarrassed and he laughed. It was like he already knew.

"Oh, come on, it can't be that bad, Scarlett."

"It's not that it was bad. It was just embarrassing given the situation I'm in now. Just like any little girl, I wanted to be a... princess."

He let out a loud laugh and I sighed. It was not that funny.

"I'm serious! My mom would sew me these dresses and I would go around the house acting like I was better than everyone, even though I looked like a hot mess."

Christian grinned at me. "Cute... Well, it looks like your wish came true."

I laughed. "Seems so, but it's way better than I could have imagined. I'm a soon-to-be queen instead."

He reached across, grabbing my hand when his phone rang again.

"It might be important," I said, and he just shook his head.

"My beta can survive a couple hours without me." he turned his phone off, setting it aside.

I finally picked up my glass of wine, taking a sip. "I'm not a big wine person, but this is amazing,"

"I know, it's one of my favorites."

As we waited for our food, we fired questions at each other back and forth, just getting to know one another better. When the food came, I had to admit, it looked amazing and tasted even better.

"I told you!" he stated, with a proud look on his face.

I rolled my eyes. "Are you ever wrong?"

"Not really."

I snorted, shaking my head.

"Christian!" We both turned and saw his beta walk up quickly.

Christian immediately stood. "What's wrong?"

"It's the sectors. They were attacked." he rushed out and my heart dropped as tears glossed my eyes.

Christians eyes drifted to mine.

"Which sectors?! What letter?" I asked. Please don't be C.

"All of them."

A sob ripped through my chest. "W-we have to go," I said, standing up.

"Scar..."

"I don't care! One of those is my sector! I have to see if my family is okay!" I tuned them out as I marched towards the doors of the restaurant. "Please, Goddess, don't take them from me." I sobbed out.

CHAPTER EIGHTEEN

◆◇◆

Scarlett

The gut-wrenching feeling in my stomach didn't go away through the long drive to the sectors. I looked down at my shaking hands and my heart raced. My mind was everywhere. I didn't know what to believe, to think— to assume.

I felt Christian rest his hand on my thigh and I looked over with teary eyes. He drove silently, leaving me in peace to think.

"We can do this," he reassured, and I closed my eyes, feeling a tear drop down my cheek. I didn't know if he was trying to convince me or himself.

I just nodded, looking up and seeing the gates now coming into sight. Guards followed behind us in many cars. Ambulances were pouring from the gates one after another. I had to cover my mouth to hold in a sob. *This was not the place I grew up in.*

As we entered the sectors, my heart finally felt like it might burst into pieces as I looked at all the families crying, and bodies scattered. I watched as a little girl, no older than four, wept as the paramedics tried to clean her up.

We turned onto a familiar road and people started gathering once they saw the sleek vehicles and the royal symbol on them. Once we parked, I felt like I was going to get sick. The windows to my family's house were shattered, glass laid on the ground. The door looked like it had been kicked in, and the fence around the house had also been torn down to pieces.

Once we stepped out of the car, Christian was by my side instantly. People cried out to their King as we walked towards the house. They needed comfort— something. I had to block out the horrid screams and cries. The glass crunched beneath our feet as we made our way inside.

"Madre?" I called out with a shaky voice. "Papa?"

We walked to the living room and I quickly turned into Christian's chest as sobs escaped. His hand was placed on the back of my head and the other around my waist, holding me close to him.

Blood was everywhere. It was against the walls, on the floor, and even on the ceiling. This wasn't the home I knew.

"Has any of the Queen's family been seen?" Christian asked someone behind us.

"No sir, but some royal guards are missing. We saw them guarding the house last. We think they may have gotten the Queen's family out and to safety." My heart leaped with joy hearing that news.

"Get our best trackers on it now."

I looked up at Christian who cupped my face gently. "We're going to find them, even if I have to go look for them myself."

I nodded numbly. This didn't seem real.

We started to walk out onto the porch and saw many people from all sectors gather around hesitantly, wanting to hear something from their king. Christian looked around, thinking about what he was going to say.

"The hunters have crossed a line. They not only hurt my mate, but they hurt my people, an important part of me. If I have to enter the war myself to end it, I promise to you all, I will get revenge we deserve. Nothing can make up for the loss of your loved ones, but closure can be a start. I promise you all, I will end this. I will personally see to it that you all have a safe place until the war is over. That is why I have contacted all alphas whose packs are waiting with open arms. All sectors will be dispersed into different packs for the time being."

Gasps were heard from every direction and seconds later, cheers of happiness.

"May the Goddess be with you all," he completed, and we headed back towards the cars with our heads held high.

We had to be strong.

***

I stared at the field as the flowers moved gently in the breeze. The scent crept through my nose, relaxing me. I'd been here for hours, just thinking. I waited for a sign, for a message, for absolutely anything, but nothing came.

The sound of someone approaching caught my attention and I turned to see someone I could really talk to right now.

"Oh, girly," she said, sitting next to me, pulling me to her.

"I came right as I heard," Octavia said softly and I tried to hold back the tears that filled my eyes.

"I'm so sick of crying," I mumbled.

"Sometimes it's best to get it all out. It eats at you if you don't."

I knew she was right, but I didn't want to be seen as weak. I have people watching my every move.

"I have to act like a queen, and queens don't cry. Some people lost much more than I did tonight. I don't even know whether my family are really dead."

"With what you told me about your mother, I'm sure those hunters ran in the opposite direction as they saw that flip-flop come off. I'm sure she's fine."

I couldn't help but let out a small laugh. "One can only hope," I spoke, wiping my tears. "Never mind me, how are you?" I asked, sitting up.

She sighed, laying down, looking up at the sky and I did the same.

"Well, Mason is still getting used to the whole mate thing. We fight like cats and dogs. One minute, everything is great and the next minute we're at each other's throats."

"I'm sure that's not true," I said.

"Well, I sure hope it gets better. He does have a nice sister though. I have yet to have a proper conversation, but I'm hoping soon enough we will. I need some girlfriends around there. She seems cool enough," she laughed, and I smiled, thinking about Christian's sister, Cora. I actually missed that crazy girl.

"How come the alpha's sisters are all cool?"

She let out a laugh. "They could learn something from them."

I let out a laugh, too, nodding. "Oh yeah."

"Scarlett!" I heard and sat up quickly, seeing Christian running towards me.

I stood to my feet as he reached me. "What's wrong?" I asked and he gave me a smile.

"They found them. They're alright."

A smile burst across my face as I jumped up, hugging Christian, wrapping my legs around his waist and arms around his neck. He chuckled, hugging me tightly.

"I told you. You don't mess with a Hispanic woman and her flip-flops," Octavia said and both me and Christian laughed.

"Let's go!"

CHAPTER NINETEEN

◆—◇—◆

Scarlett

When Christian and I rushed through the doors of the small infirmary, I was quick to find a nurse. "Madison," I said to her as she looked at her clipboard.

"Right this way."

My heart was acting all sorts of funny as we walked towards a room. As we got closer, I heard the shouting of faint Spanish and smiled. *Oh, mama.* When I walked through the door, I saw all three of them sitting as some nurses were cleaning the cuts they had.

"Oh, mija, tell them I'm fine." my mom said, rolling her eyes once she saw me.

"You need to get looked over," I replied firmly, making my way over to them.

My father stood up and embraced me into a hug. "I missed you, bear," he said while I smiled at the nickname he'd used since I was a kid.

"I missed you too, Dad." I pulled back, taking in his appearance. He looked tired.

"I'm sorry, Scarlett, for the way I treated you before you left. When those hunters attacked us, I just thought… if this is it… the last memory you had of me was me being a jerk. I'm going to make it up to you, I promise."

Tears brimmed my eyes. I leapt forward, hugging him again. "It's okay," I croaked out, "I was being a brat, to be fair." I joked and he let out a small laugh as we pulled back.

His eyes shifted to behind me and he sighed, looking at Christian. "I couldn't believe it at first when your mom told me, but when the royal guards showed up… I just knew it had to be true."

"Mr. Madison, can we talk?" Christian asked before I could reply.

My dad slowly nodded and made his way over to him. "Call me Allen," he said, and I smiled, praying they would get along.

"You are so lucky," Ashlee, who had been quiet the whole time, spoke.

"I am." I walked over, sitting next to her, and pulled her to my side. "How are you feeling, sis?"

"Terrible. It was terrifying. Dios mío… I was terrified."

I frowned, hugging her. "If you ever want to talk about it, I'm here," I mumbled.

"So many guards rushed into the house. It was frightening, and then, I heard the shots. We were being ushered out the back door to hop the fence while two guards stayed behind fighting off two hunters. Blood was everywhere," she confessed, pain crossing her features as she relived the moment. She looked off.

"What else is there?" I asked, knowing she wasn't telling me something. Her eyes drifted to our mom and I got the message. "Mom, I'm going to take her for a bite to eat down in the dining room while you're getting finished up."

Mom nodded and shooed us away, causing me to laugh.

"Well?" I asked once we left the room.

"I really found my mate, Scar. The guy I told you about, it was him."

I halted. "The royal guard?"

She nodded. "I think that was part of the reason they were so determined to get us out of there."

I smiled. "That's great! Where is he?"

She shrugged and started walking again.

"Why do you still look upset? Shouldn't you be happy?" I asked.

"He rejected me, Scarlett!" she nearly yelled, and I flinched at the direct change in mood.

"He what? Why?"

"He didn't say. He just did it once we got here and left as I was escorted to the infirmary."

I saw red.

"I'm speaking to Christian about this!" I said and her eyes widened.

"Scarlett, you can't force him to be my mate," she cried, and my features softened at the pain lacing her features.

"I know, but you can at least try to convince him. Maybe he's afraid. Christian can show him the perspective of the mate bond." I said and she sighed, biting her lip, a nervous habit of hers.

"Okay."

Christian

Scarlett's father and I headed out the small infirmary and down the halls of the palace. "Would you like to talk in my office?" I asked and he nodded.

"Sure."

Once seated, he stared at me questionably.

"I just wanted you to know that your daughter means the world to me, which means everything about her is important. That includes you, Selene, and Ashlee. So, I wanted to talk with you properly."

"I respect that. I can tell she means a lot to you and you to her."

I smiled, looking at him. "She truly is something," I grinned, leaning back in my chair as he let out a laugh, relaxing a bit.

"That she is. Though I should warn you, she can be feisty."

I laughed. "Oh, don't I know it."

He chuckled. "I feel you had a more important reason for inviting me up here."

I nodded. "I love your daughter, sir. I may have known her for a short amount of time, but being mates, I'm sure you can agree that it has felt like years." He nodded and I continued, "I will do everything in my power to make her happy, no matter the cost. I guess what I'm getting at is... I would like your approval for your daughter's hand in marriage."

His eyes widened a bit, but he had been expecting it. "Christian, you're a great man. I am sure Scarlett has told you about my views on the system, but you can't help what your elders caused. I can see how much you care about her, so it would be stupid of me to say no."

I smiled, standing up as he did too. "Thank you, sir. It means a lot."

He walked around, holding his hand out and I shook it.

"So, do you have the ring?" he asked, and I laughed, opening my drawer, and pulling the ring out.

"Wow... it's amazing. I'm sure she'll love it." he said, and I nodded.

"I hope so. It's been in the family for generations, a sign of royalty." I closed it, putting it away and looked back at him. "I want your intake on something else."

"Of course, what is it?"

"I want to give an important gift to her. Call it a wedding gift if you want. But I was thinking of something that would make her extremely happy and I think I know what that would be."

"Well, get on with it then," he said eagerly, and I grinned excitedly.

"I'm going to end the sectors. I'll bring in new alphas for new packs and bring back the old ones. My family has fought the church for so long on this decision and they denied it for a long time, but my father and I talked and agreed that I am the king and I will do what's best for my people. We wrote up a letter and sent it to the church, stating that no matter what they say, I will be demolishing the sectors and putting the people into their own packs. I explained the torture those wolves go through, the danger they're put in—the mental pain they experience. Yesterday, I received their response. They've accepted it. The head elder agreed it was time for a new world for the wolves."

"I-I don't know what to say. That's... the best news I've heard in a long time."

I smiled. "After this war is over, I am hoping to file it. I have to speak with my father and the Intelligence alpha about the other details, but I think this is truly going to work. In the meantime, I'll tell Scarlett about it after her coronation and then we'll announce it together. We'll slowly start to move people out, and when the wars over and the sectors are empty, we're destroying that place."

Allen grinned. "I think it will work too, but what exactly are you going to do with the people in the sectors? What about the alphas? Don't you need to have the witch that made the curses for each pack to be specified to one thing?"

I nodded. "The people in the sectors were split up into packs anyways after the attack. I feel that they can choose to move to another pack for a fresh start or stay where they are. Now, the witch that started this all is obviously dead, but her magic was passed on through generations and I know the witch to do it. She's young, but I'm hoping she'll agree." I explained.

"Wow, that's a lot to take in. Who can do that?"

"Alara Lavender, a descendant from the first of the witch kind. She is the last living in her generation."

"This is amazing."

"Indeed, it is."

CHAPTER TWENTY

—◆◇◆—

Scarlett

I marched towards Christian's office doors and was about to waltz in when it opened. My father walked out with Christian in tail and they looked at me surprised.

"What's up, babe?" Christian asked and I sighed, locking eyes with him.

"I need to speak to you...alone." I said, glancing at my father.

"I'll catch up with you all later. I need to check on your mom."

"Of course. We'll have dinner tonight, sir." Christian said and I smirked at his respectfulness. *I bet he never calls anyone sir.*

Christian motioned me in, and I followed, shutting the door behind me.

"What's wrong?" he asked.

"My sister just informed me that she's found her mate that I told you about. It's really him." I said and he cocked an eyebrow.

"Isn't that a good thing?"

"Not when he rejects her!"

"Why would he reject the queen's sister? He'd be crazy."

I shrugged. "I don't know whether to be mad or what! I mean at least he didn't stay with her just because of her new status, but what about her? She's upset and I don't know how to comfort her."

Christian sighed, opening his folded arms, motioning me to him. I walked over as he embraced me in a hug. "You're too good for this world," he mumbled and pulled away slightly, looking down at me.

"Your sister is a strong girl. We can't force him to be with her as much as I would want to. It wouldn't make a happy pair."

I knew he was right. I just wish I could do something. "Can't you try to show him the male's perspective or something? Show him that it's a magnificent thing he shouldn't miss out on?"

"It's not that easy, Scarlett. For him to reject an immediate royal family member means there is something else going on. I'm sorry, but I can't interfere."

"I know… you're right. I just hate seeing her like that." I groaned.

"His loss," Christian said and I looked up at him.

"Do you secretly have a thing for my sister?" I joked and he let out a laugh.

"Sadly, I'm already in love with a smoking redhead." he grinned, and I couldn't help but smile, he'd said he loved me.

"Hm, she seems nice, said redhead is in love with you too." I said and he smiled.

"That's good to hear." He placed his lips on mine and let out a playful growl, pulling me closer. I could stay like this all day with him. His hands on my hips, and my hands in his hair.

"I love you," I mumbled against his lips and he only hummed causing me to giggle.

The kiss started to get heated as he turned us around quickly and sat me on his desk.

"Someone could walk in," I said, pulling away and he shrugged.

"Who cares?" He captured my lips once more, deepening the kiss and I gasped lightly as he nipped at my lower lip. In seconds, he was gone, and I was left breathless.

"Your heat is starting again. My wolf is losing it. I'm sorry, I didn't realize." he said, and I looked at him, smiling softly.

"Christian, it's okay." I reassured him. "You can't treat me as if I'm a fragile object all the time." I mumbled, motioning him back over. He made his way back to me and rested his head on the base of my neck against my mark.

"After your coronation day—" he started.

"—We'll be ready."

He pulled away quickly and looked at me. "Really?"

I let out a small laugh. "I do love you."

He gave me a small grin. "I love you too. Now, let's get you to our room. Your heat will start soon. I'm sorry, but we'll have to postpone dinner with your parents."

"It's fine, they'll understand."

***

I groaned as pain hit me in my lower abdomen. "This sucks," I growled as Christian walked over to the bed.

"Scoot over." I did as I was told and he sat down, pulling me to him, "Just think, this will be your last time in heat." he pointed out, placing a kiss on my forehead.

"When is my coronation day?" I asked.

"In a week. I forgot to remind you because I've been... busy." I raised a brow.

"With what?" I asked.

"Stuff."

"Christian? What is it? I don't want you having all this weight on your shoulders."

He sighed, "I know, babe. It's just personal. You'll know soon enough."

I was about to say something, but the pain started to grow worse. My wolf whimpered.

"Cold shower time. Clothes or no clothes?" Christian asked as he scooped me up wedding style and walked us to the bathroom.

"Clothes," I replied, my cheeks reddening. *I have got to stop being so shy around him.* He sat me in the tub and turned on the freezing water. "Sit with me?" I asked, looking up at him.

"Of course." he unbuttoned his shirt, pulling it off, and undid his belt. I looked away as he stripped down to nothing but his boxers.

I sat up as he climbed in behind me and I rested against his chest.

I realized just how lucky I was to have him. Here we both sat in freezing water, me fully clothed, like it was an ordinary day.

"Have I ever told you how much I love you?" I asked and his chest vibrated with laughter.

"I don't think so."

"Well...I love you more...than...than every little grain of sand on all the beaches in the world." I rushed out, causing him to belch out a laugh.

"That doesn't even explain my love for you." he competed, nipping at my ear.

"Well...I love you more." I said out of ideas and I could practically see his grin.

"Not possible."

"Anything's possible."

CHAPTER TWENTY-ONE

◆◇◆

Christian

I smiled, walking towards our bedroom and bumped the door open with my hip as I held the tray in my hands. I looked at Scarlett and laughed. She was still asleep, and her hair was *everywhere*.

"Babe," I called out, walking up to the bed and she stirred with a low groan. "Scarlett," I cooed, and she groaned once more.

"Five… more… minutes," she mumbled into the pillow.

"I have food." I bargained and watched amusedly as she opened one eye and looked up at me.

"You made food?" she asked more awake.

"For you."

She sat up, giving me a goofy smile. "For me?"

I nodded and she grinned, moving to sit against the headboard and patted her lap.

"Eager, are we?" I asked and she giggled. *She giggled*. Cute.

I sat the tray on her lap, and she looked at it curiously.

"You made me breakfast in bed... for no reason?" she asked skeptically, and I scoffed.

"Can I not cook for my mate? I can take it back." I started to reach for the plate, but she swatted my hands away.

"No, I'll take it." she chirped, and took a piece of bacon, biting into it. "Muy deliciosa," she winked, causing me to laugh. I turned on the tv and sat beside her, pecking her cheek.

"Grazie."

"You know, our kids are going to know three languages. How crazy is that?" she asked as she cut up her waffle.

Her gaze met mine and she cocked a brow. "What? Never seen a girl eat before?" she teased.

"You said our kids," I said, and she nodded.

"Were you expecting me to say someone else's?" she joked.

"No, it's just... you want kids?"

"Of course. Don't you?" She took another bite and I smiled.

"With you? Of course." The thought of us having kids running around the palace made me grin. It's odd how everything had changed so quickly for me when I found my mate.

"Girl or boy?" she questioned.

I thought about it for a minute before saying, "Why not both?"

Her eyes widened. "So, *two* kids?"

"Why not?"

"What if we get two boys? Or two girls? What then?"

"I'll love them just as much."

Her eyes softened. "I love you."

"I love you too, Scar."

"Bite?" she asked, holding out a piece of bacon and I smiled, shaking my head.

"I'm not that hungry."

She frowned. "Why?"

I laughed, shrugging. "I'm not used to eating breakfast. For the past ten years I got straight up and went to work in my office." I confessed.

She gave me a stern look. "You need to eat breakfast, Christian. It's the most important meal of the day."

"What are you? My doctor? I'm perfectly healthy." I mocked and she squinted her eyes at me.

"Well, I'm your mate. So, I say you need to start eating breakfast, maybe that way you won't be so grumpy all the time."

I stared agape at her. "Hey!"

She held her hands up in defense with a sheepish smile. "I'm just saying, plus, whatever happened to 'your wish is my command'?"

I sighed and she grinned. "I got you there," she winked.

"Eat your bacon," I mused, and she rolled her eyes, trying to fight back a smile that tugged at the corners of her mouth.

Scarlett

After breakfast in bed, Christian left to go do some work in his office. The way he's been so nonchalant about work lately made me nervous. What didn't he want to tell me? I didn't want to be nosey and intrude on him, so I didn't ask, but it didn't make me any less curious.

As I sat in the garden, a spot that was now my go to place, I thought about everything that had happened. I was so lucky. Some people could only dream of this, and here I sat, in a perfect life. I had a man who was truly devoted to me and I couldn't be happier. I wanted a life with him. As his wife, his queen, a mother to his children. I was greedy and I couldn't care less. *I wanted all of it.*

A breeze swept the air, calming me. With the war happening, everything had been so chaotic. Octavia had called me and mentioned a few things about it. She'd been busy, too, so I didn't know much about it, but I did know it wasn't looking good. It was one of the things I hated about not being queen yet. Shouldn't I have been in on all this?

Octavia said we were moving in stronger and better, but the hunters kept changing their main locations. They couldn't find the central one. It was almost as if it was imaginary. If they found the central location, they could find the leader of it all. Just like a pack, if you end the leader, you end the community—the threat.

"You have got to be kidding me? Unhand me now!" a loud voice boomed, bringing me from my thoughts. I turned to see who it was and saw guards pulling a handcuffed woman into the palace. Her long dark hair swayed from the struggling. I watched curiously and got up from my bench, following behind.

"I am Alara Lavender! I will kill you!" the woman seethed as the doors shut behind them.

"What the hell?" I mumbled and followed up the steps, and opened the doors, walking in. I heard her and the guards' bickering as they headed upstairs.

Is she meeting Christian?

I made my way towards the stairs when a voice called out to me.

"Scarlett, dear!"

I turned, seeing Cora, Christian's sister, make her way to me excitedly. She's back?

"I have so many stories to tell you. Oh, I just missed you so much. Care for some brunch?" she rushed out and I looked up towards the stairs, really wanting to know what was going on up there.

"Yeah, uh sure. Let's go to the dining room."

"Splendid!"

I couldn't help but notice her wary stare as she looked up the stairs, but immediately a smile appeared back onto her face in seconds.

"Come, I have to tell you about my trip," she beamed, looping her arm with mine.

Who the hell is Alara?

She sure had Cora scared.

CHAPTER TWENTY-TWO

◆—◇—◆

Scarlett

I sat with Cora in the dining room as she told me many stories from the trip Christian had sent her on. No matter how hard I tried to listen, Alara's name kept dancing across my mind.

"Were you crazy?!" she scorned, interrupting my thoughts.

"Huh?"

"He told me the story about the party! You could have gotten hurt."

"Yeah, it wasn't my brightest moment I've had. I don't know why I did it honestly. I say it was because I wanted a little freedom, but I think I just said that because I knew I was in the wrong and went to a party when we're in the middle of a war."

She let out a laugh, picking up her cup of tea. "Yeah, definitely not your best moment."

I rolled my eyes with a playful smile and sighed.

"You look upset. What's wrong?" she asked, and I looked at her with a curious glance.

"Who's Alara Lavender?" I asked and her eyes widened.

She knows her!

"I-it's not my place..." she started, but I shrugged.

"Please, I know Christian has been sneaky lately. Is she the reason why?"

"Has Christian ever told you about the witch that started the whole wolf curse?" I nodded, gasping.

"Was it her?!"

"Goddess no, she died a long time ago, but Alara is a descendant. The last of that type of witch. She is currently the most powerful witch living. I don't know why he needs her, but maybe it has to deal with the whole war thing." she shrugged it off.

Yeah, maybe that's it.

"I have to go to my husband, but please, call me if you need anything."

I smiled at her. "Of course." I stood up, hugging her goodbye as she scurried off.

Something didn't seem right.

A moment later, a loud thunder broke out, shaking the palace. That's odd, I didn't know it was supposed to storm today. I walked to a window in the dining room and looked out. It was almost pitch-black outside. The winds had picked up with great speed as I stood shocked.

"I will blow this house to the ground, Christian! The audacity of you!" a voice yelled.

I hurried to the doors, walking out to the hall and saw Alara walking angrily down the steps. She raised her hands quickly, moving her hands into a fist and thunder shook the house again. I gasped, moving backward. She was doing all this?!

Christian appeared at the top of the stairs. "Alara, I just wanted to talk. Is all this necessary?" his voice boomed, and she laughed.

"I think it's quite fun actually. I hate you, Christian. I can't believe you had the courage to try and bring me here. Tell me, have you ever felt your brain turn to mush? I can show you!" she yelled as she raised her hand, causing Christian to groan and drop to his knees, holding his head.

"Stop!" I screamed, grabbing her attention.

Her eyes met mine and I stood scared as her eyes flickered from blue to black—back and forth. *She barely had control.*

"Please, don't hurt him," I said, slowly approaching her.

"You're the mate?" she had an evil grin, but Christian's pain stopped as she focused her attention on me.

"Please...just let her be. It's me you have a problem with. Don't give into the power, Alara. You're better than this. Think of the trouble you went through to get where you are now." Christian croaked out.

She just gave me a sadistic smile, walking towards me. I gulped as she circled me like I was her prey.

"Say goodbye to your mate, Christian. One mate for another. You should have just left me in that facility," she snickered, and I closed my eyes tightly when I saw her raise her hand up.

"*No!*" Christian yelled, rising to his feet.

I waited for anything, but nothing came, so I slowly opened my eyes to see her staring at me her own fear-filled eyes. She blinked like she was stunned and slowly dropped to one knee, bowing her head.

"I'm sorry, please forgive me." she whispered, slowly looking up at me.

"What?" I asked, confused.

"You don't know do you?"

"Know what?"

"You're her," she stated.

"Who exactly?" I asked, stepping closer to her.

"You're the missing daughter of my coven."

Coven? Missing daughter? My mind raced as I tried to remember why that sounded so familiar—the day Christian told me about the witch curse... he told me that a daughter of the descendants went missing.

"No... that can't be true," I mumbled in thought.

"My magic should have just annihilated you. I used it on you, and nothing happened. When you opened your eyes, they were a shining blue, you are her! You have your mother's eyes. I would know those eyes anywhere."

I shook my head in disbelief. "You're playing some mind game on me, aren't you?"

"Your mother was a witch, and she fell in love with her mate—a wolf. When she had you, she didn't make it past your birth. Your dad died because she did. The coven found your parents days later and you were gone with no trace left. You're the world's first hybrid."

My heart clenched. "Stop, it's not possible. I have a mother and a father! I-I don't even have these powers you speak of."

Christian was finally beside me, pulling me to him.

"Your mother was so powerful," she nearly whispered like she was replaying the memories in her mind.

"She's not my mother!" I yelled.

"Believe what you want, but I follow you. She was our leader before she died. I may have been young at the time, but we never forget our ancestors. Her power went to her next child in line and that is you... making you my leader." She spoke determined.

My whole—It couldn't have been a lie.

Suddenly, the day Christian and I spent in our wolf forms hit me. *"You never told me your fur was grey, and that her eyes were blue. I would have thought they were brown like yours?"*

I covered my mouth, shocked, staggering backward. "No!"

"Scar..." Christian started and I shook my head.

"I need to see my mother," I said and looked towards Alara.

"Are you sure?" I asked and she slid up her sleeve on her arm, showing a star-shaped birthmark.

"Do you have anything like this on you?"

My chest hurt thinking about it. "The middle of my back," I whispered, and she nodded.

"Then I'm sure," she concluded, and I looked to Christian who looked deep in thought.

What did this mean?

CHAPTER TWENTY-THREE

$\blacklozenge\Diamond\blacklozenge$

Scarlett

I threw her door open with a great amount of force. "Scarlett?" Mom spoke, looking startled.

"Me mentiste! You lied!" I spit, my body shaking with anger.

She looked puzzled, looking at me as if I had gone mad. "About what, Mija?" she stood from the couch she was sitting on.

"Are you my mother?" I demanded.

"Scarlett? What are you-"

"Don't lie to me! I can't take it. Am I your *real* daughter?"

She stared at me with a shocked look. "I—Scarlett..."

"Just tell me—please!" my voice gave out at the end as tears blurred my vision, and she flinched from the harshness of my voice.

"You... you're not—no." She finally confessed and I brought up my shaky hand to cover my mouth.

"Were you ever going to tell me?" I asked, completely broken.

"Yes... eventually." *Which probably meant never.*

"You took me from my coven." I accused her, but she shook her head.

"Just let me explain. That's all I ask." she pleaded while I gritted my teeth and sat beside her.

"No, Scarlett. I would never steal a kid. I was friends with your real mother's husband. Your mother's death took a toll on him. I didn't think he was going to do anything irrational. He asked me and Dad to watch you one night." She looked down as if it pained her to talk about it. "I didn't know why, but I didn't ask questions. I just thought he may have needed a night alone. The next day, he didn't show when he was supposed to and before I could even look for him, news broke out. He'd killed himself."

I felt a tear drop down my cheek. The mate bond was something that could make or break you, and I hoped I'd never have to experience losing Christian so young.

My mother raised her hand, wiping my stray tear as she continued, "He couldn't live without his mate. He gave all rights to me on a piece of paper. That is why he left you with me. He knew I'd raise you right and as one of my own. I love you, Mija, and nothing will ever change that. You are still my daughter in my eyes, even if I am no longer a mother in yours."

More tears brimmed my eyes as I looked down. "Why hide this from me?"

"Because they would find you, and they would have taken you away from me." she answered, and my eyes widened.

"Who?"

"The coven."

My mind went back to Alara. "I'm related to Alara Lavender, aren't I?"

Her brows furrowed. "Yes. Why do you ask?"

"Because I just witnessed her close up."

Mom's eyes widened and she gasped. "You have to watch out for her. She knows how powerful you are. There's no telling what she will try to pull."

"Mom, she bowed down to me. She said my real mom was powerful. What does that even mean?"

"Your mother was the coven's leader at the time. When she died, her magic went to you. That's why she is scared of you, but don't believe her act. I have seen that whole coven turn on one another. Why do you think there are only two descendants living? They were all too hungry for power!"

"Why am I just a wolf then? Why don't I have magic?"

"You have to learn magic to do it. I will admit, I had a witch block that trait from you."

"*What?*"

"I couldn't have you having a temper tantrum and blowing the house up now, could I? You didn't know it and I didn't know how to teach you! What else was I supposed to do, Scarlett?"

I guess she was right there.

"It's just a minor blockage. It's all still there. It's simple to unblock if you ever wished to learn. That magic, though, can be dark. I would never wish that upon my worst enemy. It changes you, and not for the good."

I thought back to Alara once more. Everything about her screamed dark magic: her all black clothing, the aggressiveness, her eyes— It was terrifying.

"What were their names?"

"Melissa and Stephen Bowen."

My bottom lip trembled, and my mother was quick to pull me into her embrace and I let out a sob, clenching her shirt into my hands.

***

That night, I laid with Christian in bed. My head was on his chest as he ran his fingers through my hair.

"Your coronation is in a few days. Are you excited?" he asked, clearly trying to get my mind off things.

I looked up at him with a small smile. "Of course. I have to ask, though, how will it go?"

"There are going to be a lot of important people there. You will be called forward, asked a couple questions, and then you have to sign a few things. Someone high up from the church will be holding your crown. You will walk up, kneel, kind of bowing your head, and he will start the small ritual as they place the crown on your head, thus making you Queen."

"Wow," nervous was an understatement.

"It's a lot, but in the end it's always worth it."

I smiled. "Will they know I'm part witch?" I asked hesitantly.

"No, we won't tell them. Either way, it doesn't matter, but some things are better left unsaid."

"Alright."

"Now, let's get some sleep. We've had a long day."

I looked up at him once more with tired eyes, and he leaned down, capturing my lips with his.

I knew what it meant.

Everything will be okay.

CHAPTER TWENTY-FOUR

$$\diamond$$

Scarlett

That morning, I woke up with heavy shoulders. Everything that happened the night before hit me full force when I went to take a shower and was left alone with my thoughts. I ended up on my knees, crying as the water cascaded over me.

Afterwards, I stood in the kitchen stirring my coffee, wondering how to pull myself out of this— how to get back on track. Arms circled around my waist, pulling me from my thoughts.

"Good morning," Christian mumbled, placing a kiss on my mark and I managed a small smile.

"Morning,"

"What are your plans for the day?" he asked, spinning me around.

"Nothing that I know of. Why do you ask?" I wrapped my arms around his neck, and he smiled.

"I want to take you out."

"Christian, are you asking me out on a date?"

"Indeed I am."

"Well, I'd have to clear a spot for you on my schedule, but I think I can make room." I joked.

"Hm. I thought you said you weren't busy?"

I frowned. "Hm. Did I? My mistake."

He laughed, picking me up and I let out a squeal as he spun me. When he stopped, his lips were centimeters from mine.

"Be ready by six."

I nodded and he leaned in, pecking my lips.

"Casual… or?"

"A simple dress should be fine."

I nodded and he smiled, setting me back on my feet.

"I shall see you then. I have a few meetings to attend to first." he went to turn around, but I called out to him.

"Yes?" he spun back around.

"Will I ever get to sit in on the meetings? As far as being queen goes, I know nothing about it."

"Don't worry, after you're officially crowned, you'll be walked through everything and I'll be by your side every step of the way."

"Oh, okay."

"I'll see you later," he winked and departed.

***

When the clock stuck six, I waited in a simple, yellow sundress. I was more than excited to go out.

When the bedroom door finally opened, I turned to see Christian walk through in a crisp suit. His eyes landed on me as I sat on the edge of our bed waiting, and he raised his fist into the air with a victorious grin.

"Look at you! I think I won the lottery. You look stunning, darling."

I giggled, getting up from my seat as he approached me.

"You don't look too bad yourself." I teased.

He rolled his eyes playfully and nodded his head towards the door. "Let's get going. We have a long night ahead of us."

"What have you planned?" I asked as we walked out.

"It's a surprise."

I huffed like a little kid as he watched me with an amused look.

"We're walking there. That's all I'm saying," he added, and I smiled, satisfied with the hint. It meant it was in the pack.

Interesting.

Thoughts filled my head as we walked. The moon was coming more prominent as the sun left the sky. It was growing dark and it only made me more curious as to what we were doing.

"Close your eyes," Christian said, coming up behind me, and I smiled while doing so.

I felt his hands cover my eyes to make sure I couldn't peak, which probably was a good idea. Our laughter was bouncing throughout the trees as he guided me and soon enough, we came to a stop.

"Keep them closed. I'm moving my hands, so I'm trusting you."

I nodded quickly as I felt his hands move.

"Okay… open!"

I opened my eyes and covered my mouth in shock.

The field where we came on our first run together was before me. Lights were strung up and a small table sat in the middle under the stars. Dinner was upon it and I gave him a goofy smile, walking towards him with open arms.

"I love it," I mumbled into his chest, hiding my blushing face.

"I'm glad." He pulled back and cupped my face. "Are you tearing up?"

"I can't help it! No one has ever done something like this for me!" I defended, swiping at a stray tear.

"Come on." He pulled me towards the table and let go of my hand to pull out my chair for me.

I let out a loud laugh as I looked in a small basket on the table.

"Just a small appetizer I thought you would enjoy," he chuckled as I sat down.

"I can't believe you remembered," I said, and he smiled.

"It was a small thing to remember," he shrugged, and I grinned, picking up a cheese stick.

"Oh my God, I love you." I mumbled as I bit into it and he grabbed one, doing the same.

"I know."

"What is all this for?" I asked as he poured us a glass of wine.

"We never get to do normal things couples do. You were right. We haven't had one perfect day to ourselves without something happening. I know a lot is going on right now, but to hell with it. I think we deserve one perfect night."

"Christian, any night with you is perfect."

He looked at me for a moment, just staring, and I looked down and blushed as a smile crept onto his face.

"I can't describe how happy I am. I have never been so happy before, Scarlett. I have to admit, when I was a teen, I was terrified of having a mate. My parents almost ruined the image of it for me with their constant fights, bickering, and lies. But the moment I laid eyes on you; I just knew I'd give my life to protect you. I guess some people aren't as lucky as us," he said.

"Dang it, Christian," I mumbled, looking at my lap as I wiped my eyes. I looked back up to him, but he wasn't in his seat. Instead, he was next to me—on one knee. My heart dropped.

"I was going to wait until they brought out the meal, but I couldn't. This ring was eating a hole in my pocket."

I gasped as he pulled out a small box and opened it. The ring was absolutely beautiful. Tears welled up and I looked away, trying to blink them down.

"I guess what I'm getting at is, Scarlett Rose Madison, I can't picture myself with anyone else but you. You have truly changed me for the better. Even with the simplest of things you do, each day I feel like I'm falling for you all over again. Will you do me the honor of becoming my wife? Will you marry me?"

It hit me hard as if I wasn't expecting those words to come out of his mouth. Even so, I looked back at him and smiled, nodding quickly.

"Of course, I will."

The look on his face melted me and he smiled, slipping the ring onto my finger, pulling me to him and hugging me tightly.

"I love you," I choked out.

"I love you too, Scar." I pulled back and noticed his eyes were glossed over.

Me too, Christian, me too.

CHAPTER TWENTY-FIVE

$\diamond$

Scarlett

I woke up the next morning with kisses being placed all around my face. I giggled, pushing Christian away. "I'm up!"

"Good morning, beautiful." I opened my eyes to find him smiling at me.

"Good morning, Christian." I placed my hand on his cheek, running it over his stubble.

"You're so handsome," I mumbled. "How am I so lucky?"

"I ask myself the same thing every day." he placed a soft kiss on my lips and pulled back some. "Are you hungry?"

"Famished."

"Come on, I'll fix us some breakfast." he started to get up, but I stopped him, wrapping my arms around his neck.

"I'll only let you up if you teach me how to cook your best dish."

He hummed. "I think I can manage that."

"Then after you, sir."

He pursed his lips, about to say something, but refrained—a mischievous look in his eyes.

"What?" I asked, sitting up as he stood from the bed chuckling to myself.

"Oh, nothing."

"Tell me!"

"I think I won't." he winked. "Now come on, we have French toast to make."

I huffed, throwing the covers off me. Honestly, I probably didn't want to know what ran through that man's head sometimes. It was probably something dirty, now that I thought about it.

When I made my way into the kitchen, Christian was already pulling ingredients out of the fridge and cabinets. I walked over next to him placing my hands on my hips. "Okay, chef, what first?"

"Crack these eggs into this bowl." he handed it all to me and I did as I was told. As I was whisking them, a loud knock sounded on the door.

My brows furrowed as I looked at the door and back to Christian. He looked just as confused as I was. Grabbing a rag, he wiped his hand on it. "Stay here," he ordered.

How did someone know the code to get up here?

Christian opened the door, and I heard him clear his throat. "Yes?"

"We need you in the conference room immediately." a deep voice spoke.

I peered around the corner, trying to see who it was and saw a man in odd clothing. My eyes widened when I realized it was a church official.

What are they doing here?

"Let me get dressed and I'll be there in a minute."

"You and Scarlett." the man added.

Christian turned his head, looking at me. He thought I didn't notice, but I saw a flash of worry across his face.

"Ok."

The church official left and I made my way to Christian. "What's going on? Why do they want to see us?"

"I don't know. Probably to discuss something about your coronation." he answered but didn't sound too convinced. "We need to get changed; breakfast will have to wait."

He walked past me, and I stared agape at him. *Something was wrong.*

I quickly hurried to get changed and watched out of the corner of my eye as Christian looked deep in thought.

"Chris?" my voice trembled.

"Scarlett, I don't know what's happening, okay?" he nearly snapped.

I jumped from his tone and his eyes instantly met mine. "I'm sorry, but I'm just as clueless as you are, but we can't make them wait. We need to get going."

I followed after him, hopping on one foot as I tried to put my shoes on. My heart was racing, and I had an awful feeling about what was going to happen in there.

When we made our way to the conference room and walked in, I knew I was right. Christian's mother, Rebecca, stood behind the church officials as they sat at the table.

Christian snarled. "What did you do?!"

"Sit down, *boy*." one man spoke, and his eyes drifted to me. "You too."

I quickly took a seat, shaking in fear.

"Why are you here?" Christian asked after he finally sat down.

"About your mate's coronation, of course." the man smiled wickedly.

I looked over at Christian's mom who stood glaring at me with folded arms.

The man grabbed a file, sliding it to Christian. "I'm sure you got our message. How we approved your little... project."

"I did, and?"

"Well, that comes with a price. Your mother came to us before we sent you an answer and guess what she told us? That your mate was from the sectors."

Christian's eyes snapped up to look at his mother and I saw how they were now fully golden. I reached over, placing my hand on his arm, trying to calm him.

"Why does that matter?" I softly asked and the officials let out a laugh.

"Because there has never and will never be a queen from the sectors." he stated and I visibly paled.

No...

"Yes, there will be." Christian growled.

"No, there won't. I'm glad your mother told us, since you so graciously didn't. You know the rules. If they're not from a pack, they can't be queen."

Christian never told me this...

"But you approved my request to abolish the sectors? Why?" a small gasp left me, and I finally knew why Christian had been so closed off lately.

"Because, like I said, it comes with a price. If you want the sectors gone, then she cannot be your queen. The other option is, she becomes your queen, but the sectors will remain the same and she will change her identity so no one will ever know where she comes from. We're only offering that because she's your true mate."

My eyes stung as tears filled them. "No," I gritted out.

"I'm sorry, little girl, but you don't have a choice here." the man snapped looking back at Christian. "So? What will it be?"

"Scarlett will be my queen." Christian gritted out.

"Then it's settled, we're changing her—"

"I'm not finished." Christian snapped. "And we will abolish the sectors."

"No, Christian, it's not happening. One or the other."

"Why do you hate the sectors so bad? Isn't it bad enough that they have to suffer? Now you want my mate to suffer as well? Because she's from there? Is that your plan?"

"Just abolish the sectors, Christian." I mumbled, completely heart broken.

"What?! No, not without you by my side."

I looked up at him and managed a small smile despite the agony I was feeling. "You have to. I won't be able to live with myself if I took the crown and let my people continued to suffer. It's okay, we had a few good months, right?"

"Scarlett, please don't do this."

"I have to… because you won't. This is the only shot my people in the sectors have." I placed my hand on his, giving it a squeeze. "I'll be okay."

"Then it's settled. Tomorrow we will crown Amanda as the new queen. Now reject her so we can move on with our lives." Rebecca spoke.

"I'll give up my title as king." Christian spoke and my eyes widened.

"You will not!" Rebecca snapped.

"Stay out of this! Haven't you done enough?" he growled.

"Christian, you can't do that. Please, do this for me. If you don't do this, my people will never live a life without misery."

"I will not." he stated, and I sighed, knowing he was going to say that.

"Fine, then I have to do it." I mumbled.

"Scarlett, no—"

"I, Scarlett Madison, reject you, Christian Spur, as my mate." I spoke and something snapped within me.

I yelped, grabbing at my chest, knowing the bond had just been broken, but I moved to grab my neck as a burning pain shot through it.

I trailed my hand over the skin. "My mark's gone."

I made the mistake of looking at Christian who looked completely numb. A stray tear fell down his cheek. "Why?" was all he managed to choke out.

"I'm sorry," I whispered.

I stood from my seat shakily. "I'll be gone by the end of the night as long as you promise to abolish the sectors completely."

"You have my word," the church official spoke.

I turned, so badly wanting to comfort Christian, but I kept walking without another glance at him. If I did, I wouldn't be able to leave.

And just like that, my world shattered.

CHAPTER TWENTY-SIX

◆◇◆

Scarlett

I rushed to our room, tears flowing down my face. I hurriedly started gathering what I could of my belongings before Christian came running after me. I couldn't see his face again; it would break me more than it already had.

I hated those officials with everything in my body.

After I managed to get a few bags together, I left to find my family. I was glad they stayed here for a while after the attack because I desperately needed them right now. I reached their room, barging in without knocking.

"Scarlett? What's wrong?" Ashlee asked, rising from the couch.

"We have to go, get your things together now." I tossed my bags into the floor, running my hands through my hair.

"Mija?" I heard and saw my mother and father walking out of their room.

The minute my eyes met my mom's, sobs left my body. She ran over to me, catching me before I fell to my knees.

"Honey?!" my father rushed out, squatting down next to me as my mother held my sobbing body.

"T-the church officials made me reject him!"

"What?! Why?"

"B-because I can't be queen and be from the sectors."

"And Christian just let them get away with that?" Ashlee asked, approaching us.

"No, he tried to fight back, but it was a battle he wouldn't win." I managed to get out, trying to control my breathing.

"Calm down and explain everything to me." my mother spoke softly.

After I got myself under control, I told them everything that had been said in the meeting.

"Scarlett, I'm so sorry." my father mumbled, looking down at his shoes.

"I can't believe I'm going to suggest this," mom spoke, cursing shortly after.

"What?"

"Scarlett, you're a part of the Lavender coven."

"And?"

"And if there is one thing that has ever scared the church, it was them." my eyes widened at the information.

"How do you know that?"

"Because of your mom. The church officials killed two people in her coven. She went after them with all she had. The witches they killed were innocent, but given their reputation, the church officials accused them of something they didn't do. Turns out, it was another coven that had committed the crime."

"What did my mother do to scare them?"

"She killed the highest elder there was. The most powerful person in our nation aside from the king, and she did it within seconds. The officials were terrified, so they created a peace treaty with them."

"So, what are you saying?"

"You said that Alara bowed to you, right?" I nodded. "Then I think you and her need to show up at that coronation tomorrow to take back what is rightfully yours. They don't stand a chance against two lavender descendants."

"But I don't have my magic yet."

"They don't know that." she smirked.

As I thought the plan over, it just might work. Though, what if it didn't? What if it got someone hurt? Christian hurt?

"I don't know, mom. That sounds risky. Didn't you say not to trust her?"

"The enemy of my enemy is my friend, Scarlett. That coven hated the church just as much as you do, so are you just going to leave without even trying? If the plan fails, at least you tried. Don't let this Amanda woman take your crown away from you. The Goddess paired you and Christian together for a reason, don't forget that. You can always take back a mate rejection, but you can't do that if you don't try to go and save your future first."

I took in a deep breath. "You're right. I need to get in touch with Alara."

"I think I can help with that. I did know your parents after all." she smiled.

CHAPTER TWENTY-SEVEN

$\diamond$

Scarlett

As I walked up the drive to the house my mother was certain Alara lived in, my hands shook nervously. What was I supposed to do if she said no? *This had to work.*

Before I could even knock on the front door, it swung open, revealing Alara herself. I let out a breath of relief, thanking the Goddess that my mother was right.

"How did you find me?"

"My mother. She knew where the coven stayed." I looked at the small house that was lit up under the midnight glow of the moon, and my skin crawled at the sight. It didn't give me any good vibes.

"And? What do you want?"

"I need your help." I stated.

"I tell you about your gift of being a descendant and you're already asking for favors," she laughed humorlessly. "Fine, I cannot disobey you since you're technically the coven's leader, even if it only consists of me and you at the moment, but what is it?"

"How bad do you hate the church officials?"

With a raised brow, she smirked. "Your mother knows a lot about my coven. Well, foster mother." she corrected, and I couldn't help but rolled my eyes.

"They made me reject Christian. They said that if I wanted to be queen, the sectors would never be abolished. They said a girl from there couldn't be queen, and if I stayed, the sectors would remain, and I would have to change my identity."

Her features softened. "You rejected him to save the sectors?"

"They're *my* people, Alara. I was raised there, and it was my home. I can't be happy while they are suffering, so I had to make a choice. I gave the love of my life up to save them." I confessed.

She looked in thought for a moment. "I had a mate too." she confessed.

"What?"

"I did. In shorter terms, I had to give my mate up to save someone too, so I understand."

I couldn't help but ask, "What happened between you and Christian?"

She looked away from my stare. "That's a story for another time. Now, what do you have in mind for these officials?"

"I want to go back in there and claim the throne. This happened this morning, and they said tomorrow morning they are going to make Christian marry and crown another woman. I can't let that happen."

"What about the sectors? Doesn't that defeat the whole point of leaving Christian in the first place?"

"No, the church is terrified of the Lavender Coven. If I go in there with you and demand my crown back and the abolishing of the sectors, I pray that they will be too scared to go against us."

"It's true. Your biological mother once scared the hell out of them, but times have changed. This is a big risk, are you sure you want to do this?"

"I'm positive, Alara, I can't leave without trying."

She moved aside and motioned for me to come in. "Then come on, we have a plan to get in order."

I smiled, walking in and sent a silent prayer to the Moon Goddess to not let us fail.

∗∗∗

"So, it's settled, then? This is what we're going to do?" she asked, and I nodded, my heart beating rapidly.

She looked me over and let out a snort. "Well, if we're storming the castle, then you're not wearing that."

I looked down at my jeans and t-shirt with a frown. "What's wrong with this?"

"Everything." she snickered. "We're doing this the Lavender way, darling." Alara stood from the couch we were sitting on and disappeared down a hallway.

Minutes later she walked out holding a black knee length dress. "This is what you're wearing. We wear black around here. If we're going all out, we're doing it in style." she handed it to me, and I looked it over with a small smile.

"Your mother actually made these dresses for the women in the coven. We put on our black cloaks over it, our hoods up so no one sees our faces until the last minute. It's tradition."

I nodded, standing up. "Where can I change?" she pointed to a room down the hall and I made my way to it.

After, I walked back out seeing she was changed as well. "Now that is how us Lavenders do it." she handed over the black cloak and I pulled it on, noticing how it trailed behind me as I walked.

"Thank you, Alara."

"Don't thank me yet, kid. We have a mission to complete first. Now, come on, we need to get close to the palace before the sun rises."

I followed her out of the house and down a path behind the house deeper into the woods. "Is it safe out here this late at night?" I asked, only being able to see because of my wolf's vision.

"You're a hybrid and I'm a Lavender witch, nothing should ever scare us, Scarlett."

I guess she has a point.

"Now, remember the plan. I will do my best to get us past the guards of the palace, but once we're inside and I get us to the throne room, it's all up to you after that. I'm there to protect you and get you out if anything goes south."

"I know." I replied, biting the inside of my cheek.

"Do you know what you're going to say yet?"

"Not a clue, but I'm hoping it all comes to me once I get in there."

"You better hope so, or else this was all for nothing."

"At least I will have tried." I looked in front of us, squinting my eyes. "Where exactly are we?"

"We're behind the old Malevolent Pack. It's going to take us a few hours on foot to get there, so I hope you're up for that."

"The Malevolent Pack?" I asked. "Weren't they crazy?"

She shrugged. "I thought so too, until I got to know their alpha."

"How?"

"I don't want to talk about it," she grumbled, kicking a rock in her path.

I let it go but couldn't help to wonder what her ties to the pack were.

Changing the subject, I asked, "What if they sense I don't have any magic?"

"I don't think they will, but you never know. As long as I'm with you, they shouldn't try anything. Now, less talking, more walking."

I rolled my eyes, following behind her, wondering just how exactly tomorrow will go. *Hopefully no one gets hurt, that's all I ask.*

CHAPTER TWENTY-EIGHT

$$\blacklozenge \Diamond \blacklozenge$$

Scarlett

Throughout our journey back to the palace, I thanked the Goddess above that I had the driver drop me off at Alara's. *My feet were killing me.* Little did the driver and Christian's mom know that I'd be coming back today.

Currently, we sat crouched in the woods near the border that led into Royal Territory. "We have to wait for the border patrol to come through, or else they will notify everyone we're coming." Alara pointed out.

"What do you plan to do?" I warily asked.

"Knock them out to give us enough time to enter pack territory and then we run like hell until we reach the palace, do you understand me?"

"Understood."

"Good, now they should be here any minute for morning patrol. There is exactly a two-minute break from the night shift to morning."

"How do you know all this?"

"Don't worry about," was her response.

Before I could reply, I heard voices talking and froze. I moved behind a tree, looking around the side of it as two men and two wolves walked in a group towards the border line.

One of the wolves snarled and my heart picked up its pace. "They caught a scent." one of the guards stated, looking around.

The wolves grew closer and I closed my eyes, praying that they wouldn't come near us. I heard a yelp and my eyes snapped open as Alara made herself known by using her magic to throw one of the wolves into a tree.

She walked out in plain sight, raising her hands, and then clenched them into fists. As she did, the men and wolves dropped to the ground unconscious.

I walked up beside her, staring at the four men in horror. "They'll be fine, stop stressing." she rolled her eyes and didn't think twice before darting past the border line.

I ran to catch up to her, looking in every direction expecting more guards to come out of nowhere. I pulled my hood over my head, watching as the end of our cloaks caught the wind, flapping in the air behind us.

The palace came into view and my mood instantly changed from worried to determined. *I'm coming, Christian.*

When we neared the palace, five guards came rushing past the gates and Alara raised her hands again, swinging them to the right side of her and the men went flying. The gates closed back before we could reach them and I skidded to a stop, breathing harshly.

Alara placed her hands on the metal bars, chanting something under her breath, and pushed harshly. The gates flew off the hinges and she grabbed my arm, pulling me through with her.

"Run!" she yelled as more guards came rushing towards us. She did the same thing she did to the other guards, but too many were coming at once. I growled, knowing I had to make it inside.

I ran up to a guard, channeling my wolf's strength, and sent a punch to his jaw, causing him to fly backward. I turned as another one approached, swiping my leg out and knocked his legs out from underneath him. I grabbed his head, smashing it down on the ground, rendering him unconscious.

Alara got the others out of our way as we ran up the stairs to the front doors and with the wave of her hands, they flew open and we immediately ran through with ease.

"It's game time." she gritted out.

Christian

I stood in my royal attire, dreading the day before me. It had been awhile since I'd put on this suit and my crown, and I hated the robe that draped my shoulders. None of this felt important to me anymore without Scarlett by my side. I felt completely numb after seeing her leave that room and my mother forced me to utter the words 'I accept your rejection', so that the bond would officially be over between us.

I missed her laugh, her goofy smiles, her stubbornness, and even the simple things like waking up next to her. It had been only one day, and I was completely and utterly wrecked. It took many people just to pull me out of bed and to get dressed.

I felt disgusted knowing Amanda was in her room getting pampered and ready for a day that did not belong to her. I hated this, and I *will* find a way around it.

"Final touches," my mother stated, walking into my room as I stared out my bedroom window. I turned to look at her with pure hatred as she held out the sword that was supposed to go in the holster that hung around my waist. "It's your fathers as you know from your coronation." she smiled.

I reached out, snatching the sword from her grasp, and turned back to face the window. "Get out."

"Excuse me?"

"I said get out!" I snarled, whipping around towards her. "I hate you with everything in my body and I'm trying to get my wolf at bay, but if you don't leave this second, I *will* let him out and let you see just how angry he is."

She gulped, taking a wary step backward. "Amanda will be ready soon. Make your way to the throne room. The officials are waiting."

"I'll be there when I get there."

Looking back out the window, I wondered where Scarlett was at this moment. I was notified that she'd left last night, a guard taking her Goddess knows where, and that her family had been sent to the Power Pack.

I hated seeing the tears in her eyes and the way she choked out our rejection. Seeing her grab her chest made my heart physically hurt—something I didn't know was possible.

The only person I had ever loved was gone, and I didn't know whether I would ever get to see her again.

A loud knock sounded on my door. "Now, Christian!" my mother yelled.

I huffed, making my way to the door and threw it open, letting it hit the wall with a crack. My mother jumped, backing away as I passed her and made my way down to the throne room.

"Christian, so kind of you to make it." one official spoke and I growled at him in response, storming over to my throne.

I sat, resting my arms on the sides of the throne, and looked out at the doors that Scarlett was supposed to walk through. A wolf coronation consisted of a wedding and the queen getting crowned— *it was supposed to be our big day.*

Everyone took their places and soft music started playing. I clenched my jaw as the doors opened and Amanda walked through in a white and gold gown, smiling at me. I looked away in disgust, praying this would all be over soon.

"Kneel." the church official spoke to Amanda and she did so, bowing her head in respect. "As head of the church, I gather you here today not only to crown your new queen, but also to unite her with your king." he spoke.

I felt a sudden wave of nausea hit me and I shifted in my seat.

Someone brought over a small table in front of Amanda, placing papers upon it. "You shall read this and sign your name, not as Amanda Allister, but as Queen Amanda Spur." the man told her, and I saw the wicked look in her eyes as she eagerly grabbed the pen.

"These papers state that she shall be your queen with your king until a new heir is ready to take over. Amanda will be there for her people and will make only the best choices for them. She will stand by the King's side to help guide him in tough times and to do what's best for him. As she signs her name, she signs her life to the royal family." The church official nodded at her.

Before she could sign her name, a loud crash sounded from outside. I quickly sat up, wondering what was going on. The officials all glanced at each other warily and Amanda looked behind her with curious eyes as another crash happened.

We all jumped when the doors flew off the hinges and two people in black cloaks walked in, their chests rising and falling rapidly, their heads cast down.

Though, when my wolf howled in joy at the scent that hit my nose, I knew who it was. They slowly raised their heads and simultaneously reached up to pull their hoods down.

It was Scarlett and Alara.

CHAPTER TWENTY-NINE

◆◇◆

Scarlett

Everyone stared at Alara and me with wide eyes. I looked around the room, and eventually my eyes landed on Christian who gave me a soft smile as if to say, 'you came back'.

"Get them out of here!" Christian's mother screeched.

"Go!" the officials yelled at the guards in the room.

Though, as they rushed towards us, Alara looked at me as if warning me I better not mess this up.

I raised my hands, and the guards froze before us. It may have looked like I was using my magic, but if they would have payed attention to Alara's clenching fists, they would have realized it was all her.

"You're not going to do anything." I snapped, walking farther into the room, pushing the guards aside.

"If you don't—" I cut the church official off by raising my hand again, clenching my fists as Alara taught me, while she did all the magic.

The official grabbed at his throat, not being able to breathe as she cut off his air supply. "I suggest you listen to what I have to say."

I released my hand and he gasped for air as the color started to return to his face. "What do you want, little girl?"

"First, I am not a little girl, I'm a woman. Second, if you haven't caught on, I'm here for my throne."

"You're not taking it ba—" Amanda screamed as Alara sent her flying into the wall and kept her arm raised, holding her there by her magic.

"Let me know when you want me to release her, boss, she's quite the annoying talker." Alara grinned wickedly as Amanda was paralyzed with fear.

I turned to face the church official again with a smirk. "As I was saying. I want my crown and you're going to give it to me. Christian will be my mate again, and the sectors will be abolished. If you don't, the Lavender Coven will release hell on earth for you church officials."

The man scoffed. "Alara is the only descendant of that coven, so I don't think it's really considered a coven with just one person."

I grinned as I said, "Not one, but two. Me…"

He paled, looking me over. "No… that's not possible."

"Let me properly introduce myself. Hello, I'm Scarlett Madison, daughter of Melissa Bowen, leader of the Lavender Coven." I gave him a mocking bow and I heard Christian's mother gasp.

As I straightened up, I noticed the fear on all the officials' faces. "This missing daughter isn't so missing after all, and if I recall, my mother is the one that took your first head elder out in the blink of an eye. Since her magic went to me, guess what that makes me?"

"Leader of the Lavender Coven," he spoke nearly above a whisper.

"Alara, release her." I ordered and she did, letting Amanda drop to the ground with a thud. "That'd be correct," I tilted my head to the side. "So, what's it going to be, Mr. Official?"

He looked back at the others who all seemed to be in a panic. He sighed, holding his hand out. "Bring me the crown," A breath I didn't know I was holding left me as someone brought him the queen's crown.

"We accept your terms." he growled out. "Now kneel, so I can crown you."

I hummed as I walked before him but remained standing. I reached out, snatching the crown from his hands, and looked him in the eyes as I placed it on my head.

"Kneel before your queen." I commanded and looked to Christian's mother. "You too."

They both clenched their jaw and slowly dropped to one knee, bowing their heads. I turned and faced the other officials and they slowly did the same.

"That's my girl," I heard and saw Christian grinning at me.

I winked at him as I walked over to the papers that laid on the small table and leaned down, looking them over. I kept my composure as I grabbed the pen. "Queen Scarlett Spur," I spoke as I signed.

I stood, walking up the stairs to the throne next to Christian and slowly sat down, feeling relief wash over me. Alara grinned, walking up next to me, and took a protective stance at my side.

"As queen, I will abolish the sectors, and I will get people into packs they rightfully belong in. Then, I will aid Christian and Alpha Mason in war so that we can have a victory for us wolves." I called out, and looked over at Christian who nodded at me, a proud smile on his face.

"You're dismissed." Christian added.

Everyone was quick to rush out of the room and I let out a laugh at their scared selves.

"This was fun," Alara snickered as she watched. *Indeed, it was.*

CHAPTER THIRTY

---◆◇◆---

Scarlett

"Take care of yourself, alright? I'll see you soon." Alara smiled, placing her hand on my forearm.

"Thank you for everything, Alara, this wouldn't have been possible without you." I stated, and she gave me a small shrug.

"No big deal, I just committed treason with you by storming the palace." she mused. "Scarlett, if you ever remove your blockage, I think you're going to be a great witch. I also think you're going to be a great queen."

"That means a lot to me, thank you. You're not as bad as everyone makes you out to be." I admitted.

She looked down, as if it pained her to hear me say it. "Yeah, don't think that just yet." she mumbled. "I'm not the person you seem to think I am."

"Care to elaborate?"

"I…" she trailed off as she saw Christian approach us.

"Leaving?" he asked her, and she looked away.

"Yeah, I'll be back soon though to help you."

His brows furrowed. "So, you've changed your mind? You're going to help me?"

"Not for you… for her." she smiled at me, spinning on her heels, and walked out the doors of the palace.

Christian watched her leave with a confused look. "What is it with you and her? What happened?"

He turned to face me. "We need to talk. Let's go to my office."

I watched him head for the stairs and I shook my head. Why would neither one talk about it?

Once we made it into the office, Christian was quick to pull me into his embrace. "I'm so damn glad you did what you did today."

I wrapped my arms around him, holding him tightly, never wishing to let go. "I couldn't give up without trying."

"Well, I'm glad you did. Now, can you take back your rejection please so things can go back to normal?"

I smiled, straightening my posture. "I, Scarlett Madison, take back my rejection and accept you, Christian Spur, as my mate." we both sighed in relief as the familiar feeling of our bond appeared, though it didn't feel the same.

Christian must have seen the confused look on my face. "I'll have to remark you soon. Then everything will feel as it did before,"

"Oh, I forgot." I mumbled, running my hand over the bare skin where my mark used to be.

"Now, what I needed to talk about…" he trailed off, walking to his desk, and picked up a file, handing it to me.

"Look this over and tell me what you think." I grabbed it, opening it as I scanned its contents.

"Is this?"

"Alphas I'll be bringing up with the help of Alara. That's why I originally brought her here, but that day turned into a chaotic disaster."

"Well, it turned out for the best." I snorted.

"That's very true…"

I glanced back down at the papers, reading them carefully.

Oliver Fitzgerald, age twenty-six. Oliver is a great man, with a great reputation for being a philanthropist. Background check looks good, and he's the perfect candidate for an alpha. If he accepts, he'll be the new alpha of the Immaculate Pack.

There were other notes Christian made about him and why he would be fit as an alpha, but I skimmed over them as I read the other names.

Adrian Lee, age twenty-eight. Related to the alpha of the Rampant Pack 'George Lee' from previous generations. Adrian is loved by many and is the CEO of his own business.

Evan McConnell, age twenty-seven. Previous alpha of the Malevolent Pack. We negotiated and came to an agreement that he can have his alpha title back as long as the Malevolent Pack remains harmless. He will aid the queen and king when ordered to do so. The deal for him to agree was that he gets his mate back, Alara Lavender.

I quickly covered my mouth. "I knew something was up!"

"What?" Christian asked, peering over at what I was reading.

"Alara, she mentioned she knew the alpha of the Malevolent Pack, but I had no idea they were mates. Though, she did tell me she had one. I should have put the pieces together…" I mumbled, but then reality sank in.

"The Malevolent Pack?! Are you serious?! They killed people, Christian." I scolded. "I thought they were done for and you took down their alpha? Now I know where their dark magic came from, it was Alara!" I couldn't believe it.

"I did stop their alpha. Evan is a powerful man, but I stripped him of his title and banished him to the cells. It's a long story, but I had a witch put a spell on him when I first went up against him. With the snap of my fingers, he's dead. He's submissive to me. Do you want to know how I stopped Alara, though?"

"How?"

"I killed him in front of her." my shaky hand covered my mouth.

"Christian, you didn't…"

"It snapped their bond, and it weakened her, and I was finally able to get through to her. I explained the spell I put on him, and if she agreed to get help, with the snap of my fingers I could bring him back. Why she got involved with dark magic, I never knew, but I put her in a facility to get that out of her and turn her back into the kind woman she once was."

"Were you successful?"

"I brought him back to life and put him in the cells while she went to a facility to get help. While he was in the cells, he had to be deprived of the black magic she used on him as well to get better again. The Malevolent Pack never used to just kill for fun before them two. They just never showed mercy to enemies and so everyone feared them, but Alara and Evan changed that. They were ruthless."

"Why not send him to the same facility? Why banish him to the cells?"

"Because it took so many witches to even weaken her. She had to be alone or that black magic would have killed anyone in her path, maybe even including her mate. If I didn't keep him in the cells, he would have gone after her and done Goddess knows what. It's not my proudest moment, but I had my people to think of."

As I took in the information, I realized why Alara helped me. When she told me she also had a mate and had to give him up to save someone, that someone was herself. She knew if she didn't, she'd never see him again. She had to get better, and I believe she had.

"I know she did horrible things, but she doesn't seem that way now."

"I know, but I can't one hundred percent trust her yet. Black magic twists your mind and some days you don't even know who you are, so this is why I'm giving them another chance to redeem themselves."

"Well, she's starting to earn mine." I confessed. "Sure, she tried to kill me, but knowing how I felt when the church took you away from me, I could have killed them too. She was hurt seeing you again after what happened. It reminded her of losing her mate."

"I think her helping you today was her trying to regain that trust, and if she continues to stay away from black magic, I think she can do some good with her life."

"Agreed. When are you bringing up the new alphas?"

"I'll be calling them tomorrow. If they accept, then they will come here the day after. We also have to make you officially queen."

"I thought I already was?"

"You are, in the churches eyes, but you have to do the bonding ritual with me so that your wolf can be sensed by all wolves as Luna and Queen of the Royals."

"Oh, okay. Sounds easy enough."

"It's not a long process, but it needs to be done."

"So, what now?"

He grinned as he said, "Now we can have a night to ourselves as mates, and tomorrow we celebrate you as Queen. Are you hungry?"

"Starving," I replied, and he stuck his hand out.

"Come on, let's go get some dinner, it's been a long day"

CHAPTER THIRTY-ONE

$$\bullet\!-\!\!\!\diamond\!\!\!-\!\bullet$$

Scarlett

I nervously stood by Christian as the camera was getting fixed up before us. We both stood in royal attire, crowns upon our heads. It felt so odd. The corset of my dress was smothering me, and I felt like I was going to pass out any minute. Christian woke me up bright and early telling me we had to do a national broadcast.

"You're on in three...two...one!" the guy behind the camera motioned for us to start speaking.

"Good afternoon. I am here today with your new queen, Scarlett Spur, to address an issue that has come to my attention. The sectors have been attacked and ruined, so many of you are questioning when they will be back up and running. The answer is never."

I smiled at the camera, knowing the wolves from the sectors were howling with joy.

"We're ending the PS system. I am bringing up new alphas and plan to continue with new packs. People of sectors can stay in the pack they are in now or move to new ones as the others are built. That applies to people in packs, too. Feel free to move where you desire." Christian wrapped an arm around me and smiled.

I took a deep breath before speaking. "I'm not ashamed to announce that I was from the sectors. This might come as a shock to you, but I'm here to say that this is happening, and nothing can change our decision. This could be a new change in the war, and this could change everything. No more separation. Today, we unite as one: a nation reborn," I declared, and Christian nodded in agreement.

"More news will be given later on this week. Have a good day, and may the Goddess bless you all."

The camera cut off and I sighed, turning to Christian.

"See? It wasn't that bad," he pointed out.

"You're a blunt person. You didn't even ease into it. You were just like 'we're ending it all'," I said in a deep voice and he let out a laugh.

"Sometimes being blunt is the best way," he shrugged.

"Well, I can't breathe, and I like feel my lungs are going to be crushed from this corset."

"Well, you're going to have to wait a little longer. We have a celebration to get to," he winked.

He took my hand, leading us out of the throne room and down the hall where the ball room was being held. I heard the chatter from inside and I grinned up at him. *This was real...* we were King and Queen finally.

"After you, my queen."

I blushed, pushing open the doors and walked in. All attention turned towards us and we waved, walking farther into the room.

"Thank you for all coming to celebrate my mate, it means a lot to the both of us. Please, feel free to come and introduce yourselves. Enjoy yourselves and we look forward to talking with some of you!" he told everyone, and cheers broke out.

I felt all giddy as I walked around, my gold dress shining under the lights of the ball room.

"I knew you could do it." I turned to see my mother, father, and sister walking up to us.

I couldn't help but tear up as I practically threw myself into my mother's arms. "I did it, mom."

"I know, mija, I know." she cooed, rubbing my back.

I pulled back, letting out a small laugh, and wiped my tears. I hugged Ashlee and my father before asking, "Did Christian call you all?"

"Yes, he wanted to surprise you. Though, I was surprised you didn't yourself." my mom narrowed her eyes and I gave her a sheepish smile.

"I'm sorry, so much has happened that I haven't really had a chance to let all this sink in. I was terrified when Alara and I started to make our way here, but the minute I reached the castle, I knew I had to give it my all."

"I'm just teasing you; I know that this is all a lot to take in. Considering what you managed to do yesterday, I'm so proud of you. Not many people would have the guts to stand up to the church like that."

"You sure showed them," my father winked.

I looked over at Ashlee who was staring across the room at someone. I followed her eyes, seeing she was staring at a guard that was standing by the main doors. My heart hurt for her as I realized that he must be her mate who rejected her.

As I looked him over, I noticed the small wedding band on his left hand. He was married. He already had someone he loved.

"Ashlee, are you hungry?" I asked, changing the subject before my parents caught on to what we were looking at.

"Sure," she tried to manage a smile.

I looked over at Christian who had left us to our conversation and started his own with someone close by.

"Come on, let's go get something to snack on. Mom, dad, feel free to do as you please. I'll be back in a minute." Ashlee and I walked away, and I placed my arm around her shoulder, pulling her to me.

"I'm sorry, Ashlee. I know that it must be hard seeing him here."

"It is, but I understand why he did it."

"So, you knew he was married?"

"I just noticed it. I guess I was so caught up in the moment in actually finding my mate that I didn't bother to pay attention to his wedding band. I'm glad he's happy, though, I really am." the hurt that was prevalent on her face made me frown.

"You know, there's always a chance to have a choice mate or second chance mate. You never know what the Goddess has in store for you." I reminded her.

"I know, but that still doesn't make it hurt any less." I rubbed her back as we approached the table full of different finger foods.

"I don't think I'm so hungry after all, so I just think I'm gonna go sit down."

I sighed, nodding. "Okay, let me know if you need anything."

She gave me a thumbs up before leaving to take a seat at a nearby table.

"I assume she's not taking it too well?" I heard Christian ask.

He walked up next to me, wrapping an arm around my waist. I leaned my head against his shoulder as I stared after her. "No, and I hate seeing her like this."

"When you rejected me, I felt this horrible pain in my chest. My wolf went silent— numb even. It made me sick to my stomach, and when you left and I had to accept your rejection, I had to excuse myself to go and be sick. It drains you— mentally and physically."

"I'm so sorry, Christian. I only did it because I knew you wouldn't, and you were the last chance at saving the sectors."

"I know, but I hated having to accept that. I'm just glad you came back." he smiled down at me.

"Me too," I leaned up, pressing a kiss to his cheek. "But we're together now, there's nothing holding us back."

"You're right about that."

I looked around. "Did Octavia and Mason not come?"

"No, they had some stuff they had to do, but they told me to tell you that they wish you the best of luck as Queen. Octavia also said something along the lines of 'tell her she better continue showing the church what's up. No one messes with my best friend like that.' And some other things that aren't appropriate for me to repeat here."

I belched out a laugh, shaking my head. "I'm sure she did. I miss that girl."

"Everyone looks to be having a good time." Christian pointed out and I looked over to see my mother and father laughing as they chatted with some people around them.

"I guess so,"

Christian looked over at me with a sly grin. "Mrs. Spur, would you like to get out of here?"

I raised a brow. "Depends on what you have in mind."

He gave me a shrug. "I guess you'll have to find out."

"We have people to talk to," I giggled.

"This will go on all night; we can slip away for a few."

"Well, when you put it like that…" I placed my hand in his, laughing as he pulled me through the crowds of people and slipped us out the back door.

"Christian!" I giggled as he pulled me quickly down the hall. "Where are you taking me? We can't be gone too long, we're the guests of honor!"

"The ball isn't important, but what is important is what I'm about to show you," he grinned.

I struggled to keep up with his pace, but considering how excited he looked, I'd run miles to continue to see that.

"Chris! Just tell me," I laughed as we ran up some stairs.

"We're almost there. Just hold on."

We went up a floor and he walked us to a door that led outside to a balcony. After opening the doors, he walked us out and I looked around in confusion.

"What are we doing out here?" I asked as he pulled me to his chest.

"I know we didn't get the wedding we hoped for. Wolves' coronations serve as a wedding as well, as you know, and I was upset that you didn't get the day you deserved. I know it isn't much, but I got you a wedding present you could say." he replied, and I frowned.

"Christian, I don't care that we didn't have a proper ceremony. What matters is that at the end of it, we get to be together. You didn't have to get me anything."

"I couldn't resist. Plus, it's small."

I rolled my eyes but couldn't help but smile. "Okay, fine. What is it?"

He pointed up and I looked up confused. "Huh?"

"I bought you a star."

"You bought me a star?! Which one?!" I looked eagerly and he chuckled, pointing to one.

"Right there… I think. I'm honestly not one hundred percent certain because there are a lot of them, but I believe that is the one."

I looked to where he was pointing and raised my hand to point as well. "That one?"

"I think so, from what I remember."

"Christian, that's so sweet of you. I love it."

"I did it so that any time we're apart, you can always look up at our star."

I gave him a small grin. "You're so cheesy."

"Only for you."

I leaned up, pressing my lips to his and I went to pull away, but instead he deepened it, holding my waist so I couldn't back away. After a minute, he pulled back and his eyes were shining a bright gold as his thumb ran across my cheek.

"You're so beautiful," he mumbled, his eyes not leaving mine.

"I don't know what I would do without you."

His smile widened as he leaned back in for another kiss. This time, the kiss was full of love and passion. It felt as if I let him go, he'd simply vanish.

He broke the kiss, sweeping me up in bridal style and looked at me with heated eyes. "Care to miss a few more hours of the ball?"

I thought about it and placed my hand on his cheek. "You don't have to ask me twice." he bit his lip to hold back his smirk and quickly turned, walking us back inside.

It didn't take long until we were back in our room. He placed me on my feet, pulling off the suit to his jacket. "Are you sure about this? We don't have to."

"I want to," I breathed nervously, walking up to him.

As I started to unbutton his shirt, he pressed his lips back to mine with a new hunger to them. His hand went around to work on untying the strings of my dress.

I pushed his shirt over his shoulders, letting it fall to the floor as he picked me up, walking me back to the bed.

When he laid me down, he stared into my eyes with a serious look. "I love you, Scarlett Rose Madison."

"I love you too, Christian Dimitri Spur."

CHAPTER THIRTY-TWO

$$\bullet\!\!-\!\!\diamond\!\!-\!\!\bullet$$

Scarlett

Christian and I stared at one another as he trailed a hand down my cheek. "How do you feel?"

I blushed, looking away from his stare. "Good..."

He chuckled, his arm snaking around my bare waist and pulled me closer. "There's no need to be shy now."

I rolled my eyes at him, placing my head on his chest. He grabbed my hand, brought it to his lips, and placed a soft kiss on the top of it. "I just wanted to make sure you felt alright."

"I'm more than alright,"

I could practically see him smirking as he said, "Yeah? Well, that's good to know."

I snorted, moving out of his grasp, and slowly sat up, bringing the sheet to cover my chest. "We need to go back downstairs before people begin to wonder where we've ran off to."

He sighed. "I know, as much as I just want to lay here with you where it's peaceful, you're right." he sat up, getting up from the bed and I watched as he started to dress.

I winced, getting up as well, and started to slip back into that tight dress I despised. *Stupid corsets.*

"Tie me up?" I asked, turning my back to him.

I heard him walk over, and his hand grabbed the strings. A shiver ran down my spine as his hands touched my bare back.

"All done," he whispered. "I'm glad my mark is back upon your neck." he mumbled, trailing his fingers along it.

"We need to get going," I reminded.

I turned to face him, and he leaned down, placing one last kiss on my lips. "You may want to fix your hair first," he mused.

I quickly turned and walked to the bathroom, looking in the mirror. I stared in horror at my hair that stuck out in every direction. Goddess, I looked like a mess.

I grabbed a brush, trying to comb it down to look somewhat presentable. My makeup was smudged in some parts and I tried my best to fix it. Though, I was definitely not as good as my makeup artist from this morning.

"Ready?" Christian asked as I walked back out.

I nodded, following him to the bedroom door. When he opened it, we halted, seeing a man standing there as if he were about to knock on the door.

"Dad? What are you doing up here?"

"I just got back from my trip and wanted to talk to you."

"I have nothing to say to you. Do you know what mom did to us?"

His father sighed, "I heard... I'm sorry, Christian."

"Are you? Because if you were, you would have been there to stop it."

"Even if I was there Christian, I couldn't have said anything that the church officials would have listened to."

"You told me she'd make a great queen and Luna! Then you just disappear when we need you the most?"

"Christian, if you knew—"

"As you always say! If I knew, I would understand, yet you never bother to elaborate on exactly, do you?"

"You two come with me. Your mother and I need to speak to you. To explain everything."

Christian scoffed. "I don't even want to look at her."

"You need to listen to what we have to say. It would clear a lot of things up."

Christian went to protest, but I placed my hand on his arm. "Maybe we should. It may not change anything, and as much as I don't want to see your mother, I'm interested in hearing whatever explanation she has to offer."

He looked at me before mumbling a curse underneath his breath. "Fine, but we have a ball to get back to, so we don't have much time."

His father let out a breath of relief and nodded, motioning us to follow him. We left our suite and walked down the hall to the conference room.

When we entered, I had to fight down my wolf as anger flooded through me when I saw Christian's mother sitting at the table.

"I'm glad you came." Rebecca spoke but we remained silent and standing. "Well, I wanted to talk to you about why I did what I did."

Christian's father sat next to her with a conflicted look on his face. "We lied about where I truly met your mother."

"Shocker. Lying seems to be your only attribute." Christian snapped.

"Just… please listen and wait until we're done talking."

Christian rolled his eyes but remained silent.

"Your mother was from the sectors. I met her when I was doing a food drive there for good publicity, and I immediately knew she was my mate."

My jaw dropped at the information and my anger finally made me snap. "Then why would you put me through all of that if you knew what I went through and how much this meant to me?!" I yelled at her, taking a threatening step forward but Christina put his arm out, stopping me.

"Because, like you, I wanted to abolish the sectors. I envy you, Scarlett, I really do. I was jealous that you managed to get further than I ever did before you had even become Queen. When the church found out that I was from the sectors, they offered me the same thing that they offered you. Stay or leave, and the consequences that came with each."

I stared at her confused. "I still don't understand why you did it."

"I did it because I wanted to test you. I wanted to see if you truly were devoted to the sectors. I wanted you to do something that I never had the guts to. I chose to stay and let them rot away because I was selfish. I loved Christian's father too much. I couldn't leave Charles, so I let the church win and the sectors stayed while they changed my identity. As far as everyone knows, I was from the Power Pack."

"How could you turn me in like that?! You not only hurt me, but you hurt your own son."

"As I said, I was selfish. I knew Christian would eventually get over it, and the sectors would be abolished. I knew from the minute I spoke to you how devoted you were to the sectors and how much those people meant to you. I knew you would choose to leave."

I let out a humorless laugh, utterly shocked at this woman.

"But you proved me wrong once again when you stormed the castle to come be with the man you loved and to save your people."

"In short, she did what she thought was best for the sectors." Charles spoke.

"You two are horrible." Christian gritted out. "Why not come talk to us? Why couldn't we all have worked together to stop the church from doing this again?"

"Because, Christian, we would not have won that battle. It's the church we're talking about. They are higher in power than us. Scarlett is lucky she's related to the Lavender Coven or else she wouldn't be here." Rebecca spoke.

"We're done here. I'm sick to death of all your lies. First it was Amara then—"

"*Don't* speak of that name." Charles growled out.

"What, Dad, you can't hear your own daughter's name? What happened to her again? What lie do you have to cover that up, now?"

"It *wasn't* my fault and I think you of all people should know that. Maybe you shouldn't have put your nose where it didn't belong."

"Don't you dare pin this on me!" Christian yelled, tears brimming his eyes.

I stared at the two in shock. "What happened?!"

Charles looked at me with an amused look. "Tell her Christian."

Christian looked at me, completely broken. "I... can't." he shook his head.

"Fine, I'll tell her. Christian stuck his nose where it didn't belong after he found out I had an affair. One that I had already resolved with his mother. He found out about Amara, and when he was king, he sent people to look for her. Someone found out, most likely a church official, and had her and her mother killed."

I stared at them in horror, something didn't add up here. "Why are you blaming this on him? And why don't you look even upset about it? You should have cared for that poor girl; she was you daughter! Affair or not, that was your blood." I growled.

Charles amused looked faltered. "You don't know what you're talking about. I did everything for them, all they had to do was remain silent and everything would have been fine. Until your mate decided differently, of course."

Christian shook his head. "I… I was just trying to know my sister. I was trying to do the right thing." he choked out.

I placed my hand on his arm. "Christian, go to our room and calm down. I'll tell everyone the ball is over. I'll be there shortly, alright?"

He angrily wiped his tears, shaking his head. "I'm fine."

"No, you're not, please just go, for me?" he sighed and reluctantly turned on his heels, leaving the room.

I turned back to face Charles. "I don't know what really happened, but you obviously didn't give a damn about Amara. If you truly cared, you would have made sure she was protected by any means necessary, and if you really cared about Christian, you wouldn't blame this on him and worsen the guilt he clearly already feels." with that, I turned, leaving the room.

CHAPTER THIRTY-THREE

◆◇◆

Scarlett

That night, Christian didn't talk much. Everyone was sent home, and he stayed in our room. I tried to get him to talk, but he wouldn't, so I let him be. I knew he was hurting, and I wanted so badly to comfort him, but he wouldn't let me.

When I woke up the next morning, Christian's spot in our bed was empty. I laid there just thinking about what was going on through his head. I was worried. The look on his face when he left the room last night almost broke my heart. He was hurting, and I didn't know what to do about it.

I eventually pulled myself out of bed and got ready for the day. I knew the soon-to-be alphas were coming today, and we would be changing history.

As I was fixing some breakfast, Christian walked into our suite with tired eyes and in his workout clothes.

"Hey, babe, are you hungry?" I asked but he shook his head, walking to our room.

I bit my lip, starting to worry even more. By the time I finished cooking, he came back out in a suit, fixing the collar of his shirt.

"Did you work out this morning?"

"Yeah, I just went for a run. The alphas will be here shortly, we need to head to the conference room when you're done eating."

"Sit with me?" I asked and his features softened.

"Of course,"

As I sat at the kitchen bar, he sat in the chair next to me, deep in thought.

"Christian, please talk to me." I sat my fork down.

"Scarlett, I'm fine, really. I just need to stop letting my parents get into my head. You think I would have learned after all these years."

"Sometimes it's harder hearing those things when it's coming from our parents."

He nodded. "Doesn't make it any easier."

"Christian, I mean this with all my heart, what happened to your sister was not your fault. You were only doing the right thing. You were trying to meet her and even help her. Don't beat yourself up because that information got into the wrong hands. You couldn't have known that was going to happen."

He gave me a small smile. "How do you always know the right things to say?"

I playfully bumped my shoulder into his. "I'm your wife, I'm always right."

"Hearing you call yourself my wife makes me so ecstatic. It's odd to think that just by signing those papers and with the approval of the church, that it means we're married."

"Well, as odd of a wedding and coronation that it was, I'm glad I did it."

He brought my hand to his mouth, placing a kiss there. "Me too."

We continued to laugh and chat as I finished my breakfast, but it soon came time to bring up the new alphas.

Alara had arrived shortly after Christian and I entered his office. I was happy that she'd agreed to help us, but I could still feel her uneasiness towards Christian, and by that, I mean the glare she was currently sending to him.

"The deal still stands correct?" she asked, and I nodded.

"You have my word," I said to her and she looked at me and slowly nodded.

"I trust you, just not him,"

"Christian," I said, nudging him and he sighed.

"You have my word," he stated, and she relaxed, satisfied.

"Are the soon-to-be alphas here?" she asked eagerly.

"They're waiting outside."

"Send them in." she turned towards the door, wiping her palms onto her jeans. I was eager to see how she'd react when her mate, Evan, walked in.

Christian looked like he was mind linking someone and soon the door opened. My eyes scanned over the three men as they walked in one by one. Alara's breath caught in her chest as she stared intensely at the last man. After a minute of hesitation, she ran and jumped into his arms, and he hugged her tightly.

"I missed you so much," the man croaked out.

"Me too," she cried.

My heart squeezed for them as I saw them hold onto each other tightly as if when they let go, they'd be ripped apart again. Finally, he let her go and she stepped back, regaining her self-control and wiped her tears.

"All three of you know why you're here." she stated as she grabbed a bowl she'd brought with her. "I need you to cut your palm and let your blood drip into this." She handed them a knife and they did as they were told.

I watched intensely as she chanted small words as the blood slowly dripped in. After that was done, she sat the bowl down on a table and started adding herbs to it. I watched as she started chanting another spell. Right as she did, thunder struck from outside and my eyes widened when blood started to drip from her nose.

"This is hurting her," I said, standing to my feet immediately.

"Let it be," Christian mumbled.

"Alara! Don't do this if it's hurting you!" Evan called out with a strained voice.

"I got it!" she snapped.

"Dammit," I mumbled and quickly rushed over, grabbing her arm.

Her eyes darted to mine and I stared in horror as blood started to drip from her nose and eyes.

"You're hurting yourself; this is too powerful for you to do alone. You may be a descendant but you're not the original." I explained.

"I can do it, Scarlett. I have to." she mumbled softly, her eyes lingering on Evan.

"Let me help you then." I offered.

"Absolutely not!" Christian snarled, jumping to his feet.

Alara raised her hand and I watched his body fly back down into his seat as she held him there. She looked back at me.

"Are you sure? You don't know anything, so I'd be channeling you."

I nodded and she sighed, taking my hand in hers. She mumbled something under her breath, and I felt as if something had been broken within me, warming my body.

"Your witch side was blocked, so I had to unblock it." she informed and turned back towards the bowl. "Repeat after me," she ordered and started chanting again.

The thunder that was present before grew louder and so did our voices. In seconds, a loud boom sounded and everyone in the room flew backward from the explosion. I groaned, grabbing my head from the impact as I hit the back wall. On the other hand, Alara was quick to her feet and let out a laugh as she looked into the bowl.

"It worked!" she cheered and was quick to grab glasses, sitting them next to it.

The alphas stood back to their feet in confusion, while Christian looked like he was going to lose it.

"Alara, release him." I called out and she flicked her hand doing so. He stood, making his way to me.

"Are you crazy?" he hissed; he was seething.

"Yes, but I feel you already know that." I focused my attention back onto Alara as she poured the black substance into the glasses.

"Each of you come and drink this," The alphas each walked forward, grabbing a glass and chugged the substance, grimacing.

She touched their foreheads one by one and said their pack's name. The alpha of the Rampant Pack eyes closed and opened. I sat in awe as I saw a pair of vibrant orange eyes staring back at me. The Immaculate alpha opened his and his eyes were a deep, but glowing green. I felt quite terrified when Evan's eyes opened and they were a deep gray, almost black.

Evan grinned, popping his neck as he felt the familiar power surging through him once more.

"Ah, I knew I always missed this feeling." he chirped and Alara hugged him and he smiled, holding her. Maybe those years did him some good. *One can only hope.*

Evan looked to Christian and gave a sharp nod to him. I think that was as close to a 'thank you' Christian was going to get. Christian nodded back to him and turned to the other two alphas.

"Oliver, the Immaculate pack will be located in Florida. You have quite a drive ahead of you. I sent my sister there who will be waiting for your arrival. Cora will help you with a few others I'm sure she brought to decide how you would like your pack to be. It's going to take time to build, but I feel you'll quite like it there."

Oliver nodded. "Thank you, Christian."

Christian just smiled and looked to the next, who I assumed to be Adrian.

"Adrian, your pack is going to be where the Nature Pack used to be held up like we previously talked about. I have also sent someone to help get things set up. Now to all of you, it will be a while before things are built and ready, so in the meantime, I'll start getting names as to who will be joining. Good luck and I expect nothing but the best." Christian completed and they all nodded.

"What about Evan's pack?" I asked.

"I already know where it is, love," Evan said with a small smirk as the alphas started leaving.

Alara looked back at me before her and Evan left saying, "If you ever need anything, let me know,"

"Likewise."

What a day.

CHAPTER THIRTY-FOUR

$$\text{—◆◇◆—}$$

Scarlett

The next few months felt like they flew by. Christian was working harder than ever on making sure the new packs were moving along efficiently, and I was getting used to my role as Queen. Alara helped us do the ritual to officially accept me as Luna and Queen. It was crazy, but the minute it happened, I felt more connected with the whole Royal Pack and the other packs of our nation as well.

Christian told me that I could mind-link with anyone in our pack or other packs and everyone would now be able to sense my authority. It was exciting, but I was still learning. I was finally sitting in meetings with Christian and learning to grasp all the new things that came with being Queen.

Anytime we had to meet with the alphas, they had always said that I was doing an amazing job, which made me happier than they'd ever realize. I was proud of myself. I was even prouder when I got to witness the sectors being demolished. It was odd not seeing a single soul in them, but after the attack, everyone moved into the packs and never came back.

Currently, I sat in another meeting with Christian, Alpha Mason, and Alpha Jackson. The war wasn't looking too good and Mason had new news for us.

"They're creating what?!" Christian's voice rose.

"A gas-like form of wolfsbane. Christian, it's already been created. They tested it last night at one of the war fronts— many men died. You can't exactly wear a gas mask when in wolf form." Jackson explained.

"Christian, you know what this means…" Mason trailed off.

"What?" I asked, unaware and distraught.

"It means the Royal Army will have to take charge with Mason's army following behind. Royals don't get affected by wolfsbane as much, so it takes a lot of it to kill them. Other wolves, like Mason's army, will die if it enters their systems and they don't get help right away."

"I sent some of my men out last night to try and scope out their lab. We found the place." Jackson said and Christian's brows raised.

"Well, that's good news."

"But it's severely guarded. I mean, there has to be at least fifty people spread out on all sides."

"So, we take our men and go." Mason stated and my brows furrowed.

"We? You all are going?"

"Mason and I will lead our men. We have to make sure this goes accordingly."

"Y-you can't! What if you get hurt?"

"Scarlett, I'm the king. Sometimes, I must take risks. If this means that I can help my people, then I have no choice but to go. I'll lead them there and hopefully take whoever down that is responsible for this."

"And if your plan fails? What if you can't get into the place?"

"Let's hope it doesn't come to that." Mason mumbled.

I looked down, worry filling my body. "When are you all wanting to leave?"

"Tonight. We have to get there as quickly as possible. If they use that gas again on another war front, our men are going to continue to die and we could possibly lose this war. The hunters keep getting smarter as we speak." Mason confirmed.

"Scarlett, everything will be okay." Christian tried to comfort. "This isn't our first time doing something like this. If I can take a powerful Lavender descendant and her alpha mate down, I can do this."

"You can't promise that, though."

He placed his hand on mine. "It *will* be okay. I'm hoping I can get in touch with Alara tonight before we leave, and she can work a protection spell out on us and our men."

"Protection spells can only help so much, Christian. I should know, I'm a witch after all. I've been reading up these past few weeks with some books Alara has supplied me with, and I know for a fact that protection spells aren't failproof."

"Scarlett, with all due respect, you're thinking too much into this." Mason spoke.

"Mason, I'm really not. I'm worried for all of you. Not to mention, Christian is my mate. Would you want Octavia going out there?" I shot back.

He looked down with a sigh. "I can't say I would, but if she was in my predicament and potentially had a way to save the wolf kind, I'd have to help her and let her do it. Think about that."

I thought about his words and an idea came to mind. "Okay, I understand."

Christian let out a breath of relief and nodded at Mason in a thanking way.

"Well, it's time to get our men ready and I'll try to get in touch with Alara." Christian decided.

As the men left, I sat by myself in the office thinking this over. I knew Christian said he would be fine, but what if something happened? I just got him back. I wasn't willing to lose him again.

***

That night, Christian came back to say his goodbyes before he left. I knew he was trying to act as if this wasn't a big deal, but it was, very much so.

"We should be back tomorrow afternoon," he said, stuffing some things into a bag.

"Okay." I mumbled, still in my own thoughts.

"Scarlett?"

"Hm?"

"Did you hear me?"

"Um, no, sorry. This whole thing just has me distraught." I looked up at him and he had a small frown on his face.

"Don't worry too much, alright? I'll keep you updated. In the meantime, you need to hold down the fort while I'm gone, okay? Tomorrow morning Alpha Adrian is calling to discuss something about his pack, and I need you to take the call. I trust you and I know you will do well with helping him."

"Okay, I'm sure I can handle that. Did you get in touch with Alara?"

"No, I'm hoping to call her again before we head out. Hopefully she'll answer." He walked over, placing a kiss on the top of my forehead. "I love you."

"I love you too, be safe." I managed a small smile.

"Will do, babe. I'll see you tomorrow."

I watched him leave with a heavy heart. Praying to the Goddess, I hoped all of them would be kept safe.

I grabbed one of my books Alara had given me and started to read more. I hadn't used my magic much since Alara unblocked it, but sometimes I couldn't control it, and that scared me. As far as I knew, when my emotions got out of control, that's when things happened.

Last week, me and Christian got into a small argument over something and I left to cool off outside, but the next thing I knew, I had set the rose bush in the garden on fire just by looking at it.

Alara said it was normal for stuff like that to happen to new witches, but it still was scary. According to her, I needed to read more about the art of control and when she had some free time, she'd come up to help me practice it.

Though, I couldn't stay concentrated. I had an idea earlier, but I knew it wasn't a good one. I didn't know much about my magic, but what if I could stop the gas? Or if Alara could? That thought alone had me grabbing for my phone.

I clicked on Alara's contact and prayed she answered, but a few rings later, I got her voicemail. I ended the call, tossing my phone on the couch in frustration.

No, Scarlett, this is a terrible idea. I bit the inside of my cheek, looking at the clock. Christian and his men were going to be leaving soon. I could follow them.

Absolutely not, my guilty conscience spoke.

I just couldn't let them go and get hurt. I knew Christian was stronger than any normal wolf, and so was the Royal Army, but I couldn't fathom the idea of that gas hurting them.

I closed my eyes, hating myself, and grabbed my phone again to call Alara one last time. "Please pick up," I whispered.

Again, I got her voicemail. This time, I left one.

"Alara, I'm sure Christian has tried calling you multiple times. I know you're busy being a Luna again and all, but we need your help. Christian and Mason are leading some of their men into what seems like a death trap." I ran a hand through my hair anxiously. "And I can't sit back and do nothing."

I was certain that when she heard this this, she was going to chew me out for it later. "I'm going to help them. I know I don't know much about my magic, but I know some. I just want to try something. Christian said you could put a protection spell on them, but I know they aren't failproof. I think I can really do this... bye."

I ended the call staring at my phone wondering if I was really about to do it.

"I'm doing this," I confirmed, standing from the couch.

I mind-linked our Axel, our second in command. **"I need you to look over things while I'm gone tomorrow."**

"Of course, your majesty. May I ask where you're going?"

"I'm going to see Alara to practice my magic." I lied.

"Okay, anything I need to know before you go?"

"Alpha Adrian is calling tomorrow to discuss some things about his pack. Just write down what he needs and tell him that we will look over it and get back to him as soon as possible."

"Of course, goodnight, Mrs. Spur."

"Thank you, Axel, goodnight."

I can do this.

CHAPTER THIRTY-FIVE

◆◇◆

Scarlett

I walked quickly, looking around. Ducking behind boxes of random things, I waited patiently. Growls, gunshots, screams, and so much more sounded ahead of me. I knew this wasn't going to go well. *Hunters are everywhere.*

I saw wolves trying their best to get to the building, but the hunters were pushing back just as hard, not letting their guard down. I couldn't spot Christian nor Mason since everyone was mainly in wolf form.

I tried to think about my next move, but soon grew scared. *This was such a terrible idea.*

There's no turning back... I couldn't.

"What the hell are you doing?!" a voice snapped, causing me to jump.

Alara ran up, squatting next to me.

"You came?!"

"I got your voicemail! You're being delusional. Christian is perfectly capable of doing this with the help of Alpha Mason. Don't be stupid, Scarlett."

"How'd you know where we were?"

"Christian told me in his voicemail. How did *you* know where they were?" she countered.

I gave her a nervous smile. "I followed them."

She rolled her eyes. "You're so lucky Christian is traveling with a lot of people or he would have easily sensed you and sent you back home. I wish he would have, actually."

"I'm not going to let all these people die from this gas, Alara." I mumbled.

"And I'm not going to let you die trying to save these pathetic men," she snapped, looking around worriedly.

"If you really want to help me, help me save them. Please."

She looked at me curiously. "Why are you so hellbent?"

"If we lose this war, who knows what will happen to our kind, that includes *your* mate too. This gas gives them that advantage, Alara."

"This isn't our fight, Scarlett. They are perfectly capable of handling this. I believe in them. You have to let them work. If Christian can stop me at my darkest moments, he can stop anyone, and I *fully* believe that. I worked a protection spell on them, they will be fine."

"You know better than anyone else that protection spells don't always work. It may help them for a short period of time, but it does wear off."

"Yes, I know, but trust me when I say, I don't mess up my spells. Look at me when I say this, they *will* be fine."

"Well, I'm not leaving," I said and stood up.

"Scarlett! Christian and I made a de-" she tried to speak, but I didn't listen as I entered the field where everyone was fighting.

Moving around frantically, I looked for my mate. He wasn't in sight and my heart clenched.

"Scarlett! Wait!" Alara yelled and I watched her as she jumped up quickly and held her hands up, making a fist.

I stood wide-eyed as I stared at the bullet that was frozen in front of me. She twisted her hand and I watched the bullet turn as she raised her hand back and made a throwing motion. The bullets flew through the air and straight into the hunter's head who had fired.

"You're going to get us both killed," she stressed, grabbing my arm.

Then that's when I saw it— a purple cloud exploding into the air. *The wolfsbane gas, they're using it on them!*

"Alara, please!" I screamed at her.

She took a deep breath and closed her eyes, chanting as she raised her hands. I watched as the smoke started to lift into the air. I then noticed a drop of blood trail down from her nose.

"I can't get it all," she mumbled.

"You can do it! Channel me!" I spoke frantically, grabbing her arm.

A yell ripped through her throat as she did so, and she raised the smoke higher and in a sharp motion, it looked as if she threw it high up and it vanished.

"There's a witch!" I heard someone yell.

Alara cursed. "Scarlett, this is not a witch's battle! You are dragging me into something that the witches will *despise* me for.... We have to go. This is not our fight," she countered.

"You forgot I'm a werewolf and the Queen of these soldiers. It is my fight, I'm sorry." I mumbled and in a sharp motion, I let my wolf take control as I shifted and charged onto the field.

Dodging bullets left and right, I channeled the new abilities I got from the mate bond with Christian. I easily took men down as I fought my way through the field.

Minutes later, his scent hit my nose, and I allowed my emotions to get the better of me as I carelessly sprinted towards him. I then saw another can of the wolfsbane explode and the cloud grew huge, and in mid-sprint, I shifted back and looked around with wide eyes.

This batch of wolfsbane wasn't just any wolfsbane.

Men that had not yet shifted clenched their throats as they choked, wolves whimpered dropping on the ground, and my eyes locked in on the golden colored wolf laying on the ground desperately crawling away from the creeping death of wolfsbane.

"No!" I screamed and started running.

I knew the only reason this wasn't affecting me was because of the power deep inside me, and I wished I could've shared it with Christian.

"Christian," I sobbed, reaching his side. His wolf whimpered, trying to move closer to me as foam started to leave his mouth and a sob ripped through me.

As his head laid on my lap, his wolf's body started to shake, and I realized he was having a seizure. His eyes met mine and slowly the color started leaving his eyes. Before I knew it, the life had left them, and I couldn't do anything other than scream.

It was like slow motion as everything stopped. The smoke was swept into the air, vanishing. My body started shaking as I looked around as anger flooded through my system, tears streaming down my face. Something snapped within me. *It was painful and dreading.*

I could see the hunters not far away holding their ears in pain from the scream I unleashed, not knowing how powerful it was. A harsh growl left me as I raised my hands in a quick, sharp motion and twisted my hands, watching as all their necks snapped to the side.

I heard small chanting and turned, seeing Alara walk up as she looked at Christian. I had his wolf's head cradled in my lap as I sat unsure of what to do.

"Ipsum ab alio renascetur," she mumbled and waved her hand over his head. He slowly started shifting into his human form.

"I may despise him, but I am devoted to you," she mumbled, removing her cloak, handing it to me. "The protection spell I put on him wasn't just some normal protection spell. It protects him from death. I put one on him *and* Mason. I wish I could have put it on every soldier here, but no witch is that strong. I tried to warn you before you took off," she explained as I pulled the cloak over my body.

"W-what does that mean?" I asked.

"He'll wake up in a few," she replied, and a happy sob escaped me.

She looked around the empty and motionless field. "This was the site where they kept the gas," she stated and smiled at me. "You can destroy this whole place. You just killed those hunters, Scarlett. There's no one holding you back. *Annihilate them.*"

I looked straight ahead at the building before me.

"And they say women always need help," she added with a smirk. "You just saved all the men. They will be thankful for you when they are on the battlefield and there is no gas to stop them. Let's destroy this place."

In seconds, the place went up into flames.

"Let there be light," she chuckled, and I looked down at Christian. I knew he'd come back but looking at his lifeless body made me nauseous.

A sick feeling hit me, and I moved over, throwing up.

CHAPTER THIRTY-SIX

$$\diamond$$

Scarlett

I sat next to Christian's bed as he laid in the infirmary. It had been hours and I was growing worried. Why wasn't he waking up?

"He'll be fine," Cora said, sitting next to me.

"You don't know that," I mumbled.

"Yes, I do. Alara never messes up. That's one thing I do know about her," she said, sighing. "You need sleep. You've been up all night"

"I hate this feeling," I mumbled, and Cora looked at me, confused. "That I feel so dependent on him. You don't understand. I felt the snap of our bond. It was like the string that tied us together ripped in half. A-and it hurt so bad." I choked up on the last part as tears started to brim my eyes.

"It's okay. He's okay," she comforted as I looked over to him and wiped my tears. "Go lay down. The second he wakes up, I'll let you know."

Glancing at Christian, I nodded. "The second he wakes," I said, and she nodded.

"I'll come get you."

***

I laid down for hours but couldn't fall asleep. I was sick to my stomach and nothing seemed to make that feeling go away. *I felt so empty.* Nothing was filling the hole in my chest. I felt like I needed a way out. Was this why my real father killed himself? The emptiness that lurked in your chest.

Quickly sitting up, I covered my mouth and ran towards the bathroom. I fell to my knees in front of the toilet as I let out what I had previously eaten earlier. I felt the tears drip down my face.

Goddess, I'm sick of crying!

My hair was soon pulled back and shocks rushed down my spine as fingers brushed gently against my neck. I turned around and saw him. Standing to my feet, I threw my arms around Christian.

"I was so worried," I sobbed out.

"Shhh, I'm here now, Scarlett." he cooed, holding me tightly. "I was worried when I saw you on that field. Why would you go there? You could have hurt yourself!" he scorned.

"I destroyed the place, Christian. There isn't that gas anymore. They don't have the place to make it nor the ingredients."

He placed his hands on the sides of my face. "I'm happy you did, but I'd rather you be alive than dead. Please *never* pull something like that again."

I nodded, pulling from his grasp, and walked to the sink, placing my hands against it as I took in a deep breath, still feeling nauseous.

"Are you feeling okay? Why were you getting sick?" Christian asked from behind me as his arms circled around my waist.

I turned, facing him. "I got sick earlier too, I thought it was just because of what all happened, but now that I think about it… I've been feeling rather odd the past few weeks."

A brow raised. "Are you saying what I think you're saying?"

I looked at him nervously. "I think I need to take a pregnancy test."

"Oh, my Goddess, okay… we can do that." he looked in shock for a moment, but it soon turned to excitement. "Goddess, what if you're pregnant?! This is huge."

I gave him a small smile. "You're excited?"

"Aren't you?"

"Yeah, I guess, but we shouldn't get our hopes up just yet."

"Right… Why don't we go see a doctor? That way we know for sure."

"That's fine, but have you been checked out by the doctors yet? To make sure everything is okay?"

"Yes, they wouldn't let me leave before I did."

I let out a small laugh. "You beat Cora here."

He nodded. "She tried telling me to wait, but I darted out of there the moment the doctors gave me the all clear."

I wrapped my arms around his neck. "I'm glad you're okay."

"Likewise," he placed a kiss on my forehead. "Now, let's go see a doctor. I won't relax until we do."

"Okay, fine."

After Christian made a few calls, we were on the way to a doctor's office within the pack that he trusted. It made me feel all giddy inside that Christian was excited about this. I was worried he would feel it was too soon, but I was completely wrong.

"Is she ready for us?" Christian asked the receptionist.

"She is, go on back. It's the first door on your right."

My heart picked up speed as we walked into the room and saw the doctor standing there.

"Your majesties, how are you both?" she asked, a bright smile on her face.

"Good and you?"

"I'm doing great, so I hear you wanted to talk about something serious with me." she beamed with a knowing smile.

"We think Scarlett may be expecting." Christian told her.

"This is so exciting! Let's get you checked out!"

After she explained some things, I had to take a urine test while she got some things ready. I laid on the bed in another room with Christian holding my hand tightly.

"If you are pregnant, what do you want to name them?" Christian asked and I let out a laugh.

"Isn't that a little too early to be talking about?"

"No, not to me." he shrugged.

I sighed, thinking about it. "I always liked the name Rosemarie for a girl and Eligh for a boy."

"I actually really like those." Christian replied.

"Really? I thought this would be yet another argument." I joked.

"No, I really do like them. I think they're perfect." he mused.

The door opened and my doctor walked back through with a big smile on her face, causing me to quickly sit up. "Are we right?"

"I'm happy to say that you're expecting."

My jaw dropped as I looked over at Christian who was in just as much shock as me. His eyes met mine and he leaned forward and placed a kiss on my lips. "Hell yeah." he winked.

I belched out a laugh. "That was not what I was expecting you to say."

"Would you like to go ahead and do an ultrasound to check on everything and see how far along you are?"

"Please," I nodded eagerly.

Minutes later I was staring at the screen in shock.

"Repeat that again…" I mumbled, my eyes not leaving the screen.

"Not just one baby, but two. You're having twins, congratulations."

"Oh…" Christian trailed off. "We're never going to be able to sleep." he added, and I couldn't help but laugh.

"No, we're definitely not."

But I couldn't be more excited.

CHAPTER THIRTY-SEVEN

——◆◇◆——

Scarlett

"Are you sure this is a good idea?" Christian asked me as I peered through the window, waiting for her to show up.

"Christian, I trust her, she has helped us so much lately. Why can't you accept that?"

"Alara was a powerful, deadly witch. She fell into black magic that nearly destroyed her. What's to say that she doesn't retreat back to that?" he countered, and I turned, facing him.

"Because she finally has her mate back. She knows where she went wrong. She knows that she took it too far. She and Evan both did, and they both paid for their wrong doings. Let bygones be bygones, Christian. It's been ten years. It's over."

He rolled his eyes, looking away.

"Your doctor said you need to be resting and relaxing for the next few days, so please stop worrying about me and go lay down. I do not want something to happen because you're too busy stressing over nothing." I told him and scoffed.

"How am I supposed to relax when a woman, who tried to kill all wolves with black magic might I add, is coming to my home to teach my pregnant wife more magic? How is that supposed to sit well with me?"

I closed my eyes. Relax Scarlett. Do not bite his head off. Do not throw something at him. *You are calm.* I reopened my eyes and gave him a small smile.

"I can feel every inch of me buzzing with power that I don't know how to control. What happens if I hurt you, or worse, what if I hurt our children? What will you say then? She is teaching me the art of control. Over the years, she's mastered it. You have to let her help me. The rest of our family's coven is dead. There is no one else left who can teach me the truth about our bloodline's magic. You can monitor the whole thing if needed, but please, Christian, let me do this."

He looked to be having an internal battle with himself, but finally gave in, nodding. "Fine, okay. I get to stay in the room though."

I nodded. "Fine, if you must," I replied, turning to the window just as a car pulled up. "She's here," I spoke excitedly, making my way downstairs.

***

"I can't do it," I spoke, almost pouting.

Alara chuckled. "Scarlett, just sitting there and waving your hands isn't going to do anything." she joked and leaned over.

"Watch what I do. I think about healing the flower. I think of the beautiful red the rose used to be. I think about the life that used to thrive through it, and boom, a rose." she showed me, and my jaw dropped at how easy she made it look.

There was a dead rose, and if I did it correctly, I could bring it back to life, sort to say.

"I've also had years of practice and a mother to teach me," Alara added, leaning up against the table. "It takes time, but I'm sure you can get the hang of it. Think about how this can affect the war! You need to have an end goal when learning. Something to strive for. It will help you get the hang of things quicker," she suggested, and I nodded.

If I could master this gift I'd been given before the war... I could help out so much. Alara and I both could.

"Alara?"

"Hm?"

"You're helping in the war, aren't you?" I asked and she looked down.

"Usually it would be a sin for a witch to help the wolves, but what I did to them so many years back... I can never be forgiven for that. I got into something that sucked me dry of any humanity, so I guess it's one thing I can do to help and to redeem mine and Evan's name. If that's even possible," she thought dryly.

"What made you come back to your humanity?"

"Evan getting taken away from me, and Christian putting me into a facility where witches worked with me to get the dark magic out of my system. I still hold the power of it, but it's not dark anymore. I hate to admit it, but if it weren't for Christian, I'm afraid things could have turned very badly. In a way, I guess I could thank him for what he did. I'd never tell him that though, of course."

Only if Christian was in here to hear that. He left after the first hour when he saw how she was truly trying to help me, and everything was okay. He told me to call him if I needed him before heading off to his office.

"You didn't get taken away like Evan though?"

She shook her head.

"Oh, I did. They just thought that Evan corrupted me and then put me in that facility that helped me through the days. Witches came here and there. I was brought back to my humanity piece by piece and the ache of missing Evan only helped. They placed a horrible title on the Malevolent Pack as ruthless killers, me as a corrupted Luna, and Evan as a malicious man."

She shook her head. "The names about the Malevolent Pack are... hurtful in a way. We are known for being ruthless, but before the black magic, it only used to be towards our enemies. Evan and I ruined that pack's name and yet they still worship us. It's a long story about the truth of the pack. That we can leave for another day."

"So, when Christian took Evan... the pack still remained?"

She nodded. "Christian put a new Alpha and Luna he trusted and knew in charge. They reshaped the pack. Created a new Malevolent Pack, I guess you could say, but not many knew about it."

"What about when you two went back? What happened to the Alpha and Luna?" I asked and she shrugged.

"Christian told them we were coming back, and they willingly gave the titles over. I don't think our members liked them very much." she giggled.

"So, the people aren't...bad?"

"No. Well... some were. Evan and I had an inner circle, and after the black magic practically brainwashed us, we ended up brainwashing them in turn. We all convinced people what we were doing was okay and that the people we went after were enemies when in reality, they weren't. I'm disgusted even thinking about it," she answered.

"Why?"

"Because, Scarlett, our family members were lunatics. They slaughtered one another for power, and I vowed to never be like them, but I did."

"My mother...was she like that?" I asked.

"No, the opposite actually." She stood up, squaring her shoulders. "That's enough for story time. Let's get back to practicing." my brows furrowed.

She didn't like to speak about her past.

"Yeah, okay," I mumbled and turned back to the flower.

Here goes nothing.

CHAPTER THIRTY-EIGHT

◆◇◆

Scarlett

Over the past few days, Alara came and went. I'd been learning quickly and tremendously. I guessed having an end goal really did help in picking up the pace. Although, today she didn't come. Something about her and Evan fighting, so I was stuck in a meeting with Christian and the one only and only Jackson Hudson, aka Alpha Jackson.

"We should use the anaconda strategy," Jackson said, writing some things down on the notes before him.

"The ana-what?" I asked and he let out a deep sigh, looking to Christian.

"Does she have to be in here?" he asked, and my jaw dropped.

"Jackson..." Christian said in a slight warning tone, but Jackson just rolled his eyes and held his hands up.

"Alright, alright," he mumbled as he looked back at me and leaned forward. "It's one of the best strategies for war ever created. If you have the means to do it and you know it will play out in your favor, it works well. In short terms, the Americans used it in their civil war they had many years ago."

"So, what does it mean exactly?" I asked, still not understanding.

"It means just what it sounds like. What does an anaconda do to its prey? It wraps around them and smothers the life out. We do that too. If we can get a general idea of where the hunters are held up and get on all sides of them, we can slowly go in and start taking over. We divide and conquer. Simple." Jackson tossed his pen on his notes as he leaned back in his chair.

"I like it," Christian said, nodding his head.

"And if the plan fails?" I questioned, earning a look from Jackson as he cocked a brow.

"My plans never fail," he pointed out.

"You clearly can't know-"

Christian cut me off. "Scarlett," he warned, and I sighed.

Apparently, Jackson and I "banter" too much, as Christian calls it. It's what happens when you put two stubborn people in a room together.

"I'll meet with Mason when I get the chance and discuss this all with him. I'm sure he'll be on board." Jackson said and Christian nodded, standing up.

"Just let me know."

Jackson got his things together and stood to shake hands with Christian. "I'll be in touch," he told him before walking to the office doors and left.

"So, what else is on our meeting agenda?" I asked and Christian shrugged.

"Everything has been taken care of for today. That meeting was all that I had on my schedule." he concluded as he sat back down in his chair and motioned for me to come to him.

I stood from the couch I had perched myself on and walked over to him. Once I was in his reach, he pulled me into his lap, causing me to squeal.

He chuckled, wrapping his arms around me. "Look at you," he said, turning me sideways and placing a hand on my stomach. "You're both already growing," he continued.

Goddess, I love this man.

"We have our appointment today to see the genders. I'm excited. Speaking of everything that happened recently, I'm glad to get my mind off things."

"You mean... where you told me you were going to stop a gas from breaking out, but failed to mention that Alara put a death protection spell on you and I watched you die thinking you'd never wake up? Is that what you're addressing?"

"Are you ever going to forgive me for that?" he asked.

"Hm, probably not."

"Well, I haven't forgotten about you coming to the field like a maniac in the first place. You could have gotten yourself or our unborn children hurt," he pointed out and I cocked my head to the side.

"Yes, but if I wouldn't have come, that gas would have gotten out and we would have been screwed, protection spell or not." I shot back.

"Point taken," he mumbled.

"That's what I thought." I grinned, wrapping my arms around his neck as he caressed my stomach.

"Please don't be pains like your mother," Christian spoke and I gasped.

"Christian, how rude."

He chuckled at my features and brought my hand around his neck up to his lips, placing a soft kiss there.

"You know I love you," was his defense and I rolled my eyes.

"I hope these babies *are* a pain in the ass," I replied, lifting my chin up a bit.

"I don't know if you realized or not, but the babies would also be a pain in your ass."

"Whatever. I'm done with this conversation," I said, not able to think of anything else and he let out another laugh.

"Got ya," he winked.

"You may think that, but you don't get any loving time from me for a while," I narrowed my eyes.

"Is that so?"

"Mhm."

"We'll see about that," he challenged, trailing his hand down my thigh.

I was quick to grab it. "Stop. You are-"

"Sexy? Hot? Charming? Irresistible? I know, love."

I glared at him.

How was he always good with comebacks? *He's been around me too long.*

"I hate you," I grumbled.

"No, you don't."

"Sometimes…"

"Lies."

I shook my head. "You're incurable. I'm going to get some lunch. We're hungry." he chuckled as I got up, making my way out of his office.

I was walking down the halls of the castle when I saw my sister Ashlee. I halted as she watched a guard from far away. He was smiling and laughing with another guard and I sighed, immediately knowing who he was. I slowly made my way up to her and placed a hand on her back, startling her.

"Hey, Scar," she mumbled, and I placed my arm around her shoulders, pulling her to my side.

"I'm sorry, sis." I told her.

No one should feel the rejection of a mate.

"It's okay," she spoke softly.

"I'm blessed to live here with you, Scarlett, I truly am. But..." she trailed off, pulling away from me and took my hands in hers. "I can't stay here. I can't bump into him all the time and feel my wolf howl with pain and my heart break all over again. It's tearing me apart," she spoke sadly, and I frowned, giving her hands a squeeze.

"I understand, Ash."

She gave me a soft smile and nodded. "I don't know what I'll tell mom, but I'm sure she won't like me leaving. Heck, I don't even know where I'm going to go. I just turned seventeen for crying out loud."

"I can speak with mom, but what if I could get you into another pack? A pack that us royals are close with."

Her eyes widened. "You'd really do that for me?"

"Ashlee, you're my little sister, of course I would."

She let go of my hands and threw her arms around me, hugging me tightly.

"You're the best," she sniffled, and I smiled, closing my eyes, and hugged her back just as tightly.

When she pulled back, I could already see the question brewing. "So? What pack?"

I grinned. "The War Pack," I told her..

Her eyes widened. "Wow."

"Yeah. Everyone deserves a second chance, Ashlee. This will be yours. Octavia, the Luna, is a great friend of mine and I'm sure that when you go to see her, she will help you with whatever you need. It may take a bit for you to get into the pack and then a few more weeks for you to get settled there and get used to everything, but I'm sure you can do it."

She beamed up at me. "I don't know how to thank you, Scar."

"You don't have to," I leaned in, placing a kiss on her forehead, and then pulled back and shot her a wink. "Maybe this is the Goddess answering your calls for a change," I said, and she let out a laugh.

"Maybe so," she said as her eyes shifted to something behind me, but before I could turn around and see what she was looking at, I felt a hand being placed on the small of my back.

"You have a doctor's appointment, love," Christian spoke and I looked up, seeing him smiling at Ashlee.

"Good evening, Ashlee. How have you been?" he asked.

"I've been good," she replied politely, and he nodded and directed his attention to me.

"Right," I mumbled. "Ashlee, I have to go to a checkup, but I'll come to see you later, alright?"

"Sounds good."

I gave her a wave as I let Christian guide me down the hall.

"I'm ready to find out the genders," Christian said and I bit my lip anxiously.

"Me too."

***

We both sat in the room of the doctor's office nervously, yet still bickering.

"It's going to be a boy and a girl," Christian said and I rolled my eyes.

"And if it's two girls or two boys?" I asked.

"I'll love them just as much." he shot back.

"Good afternoon!" my doctor said, walking in with a bright smile on her face. "Well, everything from the test came back good! Everything is looking great. We'll just go ahead and get started." she said, and I nodded with a smile.

I think Christian was more excited than I was. He held my hand tightly as she rubbed the cool gel over my small bump.

As she took my ultrasound, she pointed to the monitor.

"Everything looks perfect. They are both looking great!"

Looking over at Christian, I saw how he stared at the screen in amazement with a huge grin.

"Wow," he said and looked at me and leaned in, pecking my lips. "We're really having twins," he said to me and I giggled.

"I know,"

"You two are so cute," the doctor said, and I let out a small laugh, thanking her.

"Are you ready to know the gender?" We nodded quickly and she smiled.

She took a moment, looking, and slowly grinned.

"It's a boy... and another boy—wait, no, girl. My mistake,"

My jaw dropped slightly.

"Oh, they are so going to fight for the throne," I giggled.

"The boy has to take it," Christian said and I scoffed.

"Why can't she?" I asked.

"It's tradition. The eldest heir takes the throne. Usually, it's a male for a king." he replied, and I rolled my eyes.

"I think I've broken enough stereotypes. If she wants to be Queen first, why can't she? Plus, what if she's born first? Technically, she *is* the eldest."

He squinted his eyes, looking at me. "Are you trying to break the church?"

"Maybe.... Does this mean what I think it means?" I asked.

"May the best sibling win. Though, if he is born first, he is to be king." he said and I laughed, shaking my head.

"Fair enough." Then it hit me. "We are horrible parents betting on our own kids," I said, and the doctor laughed with us.

"You two are definitely something else. What are their names?" she asked as she cleaned off my stomach and handed me the ultrasound pictures.

"Prince Eligh Alexander Spur, and Princess Rosemarie Elizabeth Spur." Christian answered and I grinned, thinking about it.

"Congrats," she chirped, grabbing her clipboard, and headed out of the room as I looked down at the pictures.

"Hey," Christian said and I looked over to him. "So, you really want Rose to take the throne?" he asked curiously, and I nodded.

"It's time for a new monarch to break history," I said with a wink and he grinned.

Rosemarie will do just that.

CHAPTER THIRTY-NINE

Scarlett

"Christian!" I screeched as I felt paint splash onto my overalls. "I'm sorry," he laughed out.

I thought painting the babies' room would be a lot easier and a lot of fun. I was wrong. Christian was like a child when it came to painting.

Lately, he'd been the best mate I could have ever asked for, not that he wasn't before. He always made sure I was taken care of before himself. I tried to argue with him and show that I was fine and capable of walking down the steps alone, but no. He was right there guiding me down them. *Got to love him though.*

This was actually his idea for us to do the nursery together instead of having someone else do it. We would feel a closer attachment to it, he said. I agreed and was quick to start searching for ideas. Since the two would be sharing a room, we painted the walls a light green, or at least we were attempting to.

"If you splatter paint on me again, I'm shoving this paintbrush down your throat," I declared, and he let out another laugh.

"Try me," he replied, and I scoffed, chucking the paintbrush at him. Fortunately for him, it missed him completely as he swiftly moved to the side before it could hit him.

"Idiot," I grumbled.

Mood swings. Yes, that was all I'd been experiencing lately. Oh, and the cravings. I made Christian get up at two in the morning one night to fix me pizza. I had a feeling the kids were going to love pizza and pickles. Those were my two biggest cravings so far.

I felt Christian wrap his arms around me from behind.

"Don't pout," he said, placing a kiss on the base of my neck.

"You irritate me."

Christian, on the other hand, thoroughly enjoyed teasing me and making me mad in any way he could. Then, he tried to seduce me into forgiving him and it usually worked because of hormones. *Straight betrayal.*

Christian placed his hands on my stomach. "Don't you think mommy should forgive me?" he asked and seconds later, I felt a sharp kick. "I think they agree." he snickered, and I couldn't help but laugh.

They loved their dad already, that's for sure. Any time I wanted to get them to kick, they wouldn't, but the second he placed his palm, the soccer match would start. But aside from his teasing and overprotectiveness, I've grown to not be able to be away from this man for even a day. He's my everything, and soon these kids will be too.

We were scared. We've never parented before and we didn't know how it would turn out. Though, I just knew everything would be okay because we had each other. We can get through this together.

When I told my parents and Ashlee the news that I was expecting, my mother cried for at least an hour. She was more than excited, and it gave me some comfort knowing I had her in my corner if I ever needed help.

"What are you thinking?" Christian asked.

"A thousand ways to kill you," I joked, and he scoffed. "Just kidding. Kind of. I'm just thinking about how life will be once the babies come," I said, turning to face him.

"Life will be good." he replied, and I nodded, wrapping my arms around him.

"It will be, won't it?"

"I promise you, it will. We're going to be the best parents there ever was." he smirked, and I grinned up at him.

"We will, won't we?"

He hummed in response, leaning down, and giving me a soft kiss, but before it could get heated, I said, "Nope, not today buddy. We have a room to paint," I winked, pulling away and he groaned.

"Fine," he mumbled, picking his paintbrush back up and grabbed mine off the floor, handing it to me. "Try not to kill me with this." he said as I took it.

"No promises, love." I teased, going back to painting the spot I had been working on.

I glanced at him to only find him staring at me.

"I love you," he said, warming my heart.

"I love you too."

That's what keeps me moving.

EPILOGUE

As hunters gathered what they could to go against the wolves, the wolves were doing just the same. They conjured their men, got alliances, and prepared themselves for what was to come. Darkness was coming. Pain was coming. *The end of one side was coming.*

It now rested in the hands of one man to lead us into battle with an iron fist. To lead us into hundreds of threatening possibilities. *To lead us to conquer.*

We will take back what was once ours, we will rise above all like we have for hundreds of years, and we will join one enemy to defeat another.

We will stand tall and we will stand proud. We will put our trust into our alphas, and we *will* fight.

We leave it into the hands of Alpha Mason, the Alpha of War.

For he will take us to the final battle.

He will lead us to war and victory.

ACKNOWLEDGMENTS

Wow, what a journey this has been! I would like to thank everyone for showing so much support for my first book. Most importantly, I would like to give thanks to my readers from Wattpad and Radish because this wouldn't have been possible without each and every one of you. I thank my parents, Connie and Mark Harrison, for showing me nothing but love through all of this and for constantly supporting me and my (sometimes) crazy ideas. Nothing can describe how much y'all mean to me.

Next, I would like to thank all my grandparents for constantly bragging on me and supporting me. It means the world to me! (Especially when my grandmother and grandad, Kenneth and Carol Hargis, would brag about me to everyone— even their hairdressers!)

Lastly, as I know she's waiting for her time to shine, I would like to give thanks to my best friend, Emmy Parke, for reading ALL of my books and always hyping me about them. She also listens to my ideas for books and tells me if they're worthy or not (let's just say she is brutally honest). I love you, girl, thanks for everything!

Much love, and thanks again to all my readers.

ABOUT THE AUTHOR

KEYLEE HARGIS is currently in the midst of publishing her series "The Bond Series," with the Royal Bond being her first. Keylee hails from Bowling Green, Kentucky, and enjoys spending time with her friends and family. When she's not reading or writing, she enjoys videography and photography. As she furthers her career as a writer, she is excited to see what the future holds.

CPSIA information can be obtained
at www.ICGtesting.com
Printed in the USA
LVHW050310041120
670659LV00002B/117

9 781735 920702